Confessions of
a Secret Admirer

T0033892

Also by Jennifer Ryan

Chasing Morgan
The Right Bride
Lucky Like Us
Saved by the Rancher

Short Stories
Can't Wait
(appears in *All I Want for Christmas Is a Cowboy*)

Confessions
of a
Secret Admirer

JENNIFER RYAN
CANDIS TERRY
JENNIFER SEASONS

AVONIMPULSE

An Imprint of HarperCollinsPublishers

Excerpt from *The Last Wicked Scoundrel* copyright © 2014 by Jan Nowasky.

Excerpt from *Blitzing Emily* copyright © 2014 by Julie Revell Benjamin.

Excerpt from *Savor* copyright © 2014 by Karen Erickson.

Excerpt from *If You Only Knew* copyright © 2014 by Dixie Brown.

"Waiting for You" copyright © 2014 by Jennifer Ryan.

"Sweet Fortune" copyright © 2014 by Candis Terry.

"Major League Crush" copyright © 2014 by Candice Wakoff.

EPub Edition FEBRUARY 2014 ISBN: 9780062328588

Print Edition ISBN: 9780062328595

10 9 8 7

Contents

Contents

WAITING FOR YOU

Jennifer Ryan

Chapter One

WRONG GUY. SHE stopped short on the sidewalk and stared down the way, past the shoe store, collectibles boutique, and gourmet treats shop. For a split second, Taylor thought she saw Grant's face on another man. Happened to her all the time. Every time her gut tightened with anticipation and turned to stone with profound disappointment when she discovered it was just her mind playing tricks on her again. Besides, he wouldn't want to see her anyway.

The familiar face in question turned to her. Grant's brother, Seth, stood on the sidewalk with a little girl atop his shoulders. The smile Taylor remembered from days gone by. It notched up to megawatt when he spotted her. The initial tidal wave of unease at seeing him for the first time in more than eight years dissipated into flutters. Like him, she weaved her way through the other people shopping and going to dinner downtown. The twinkling lights wrapped around and up the tree trunks and bare branches lining the street faded as Seth drew closer. She dismissed their cheerful glow, like she'd dismissed Christmas a few weeks ago. She didn't want to think about that lonely couple of days.

"Damn, Taylor, you're even more beautiful than I remember. How are you?"

"That one's a dollar, Daddy," the princess piped up, holding out her small hand. Seth dug in his pocket and pulled out the cash and slapped it into her palm with a good-natured grumble.

For the first time since she came back home to Fallbrook, she smiled.

Taylor leaned up and accepted the peck on her cheek. "I'm just fine." She gave Seth's wide shoulders a squeeze before stepping back and gazing up at the child holding onto his head. "Looks like time's been sweet to you. Who's this?"

"My five-year-old, Maggie." Seth smiled up at his little girl and she beamed a matching smile down to him. "Maggie, this is Taylor, a very good friend from high school."

"It's nice to meet you," Taylor said, waiting for the old hurt to rise up, but it didn't. Maybe this is how things were always meant to be. That thought shifted her memories of the past and changed the way they looked. Old hurts and disappointments turned to sweet memories of puppy love and random acts of recklessness. "That's the prettiest tiara I've ever seen."

"I'm a snow princess." Maggie beamed.

Taylor settled her gaze back on Seth's face; his eyes were alight with pride. "She's beautiful."

"Like her mother," he said automatically. She caught a glint of unhappiness in his eyes that told her while his daughter may be the sparkle in his eye, his wife had lost some of her shine.

At one time, a long time ago, that might have made her happy. Not now. She'd moved on. Seeing him with his daughter and the gold band firm on his finger made her understand that sometimes good-bye has a lot more good in it than she'd thought when she caught him cheating.

Well, maybe it wasn't cheating at all. They'd always made better friends than anything more. Another girl had turned his head, and Taylor discovered her heart belonged to someone else. Someone she'd never thought would ever look at her in that way, until he did.

"How's the family?" What she really wanted to ask was, "How is Grant?"

She didn't, but held her breath and hoped he'd say something, anything about his older brother. Who'd avoided her like the plague since she'd returned nearly a month ago.

"Everyone is great. Amy is in the diner with my other daughter, Millie, getting hot chocolate." His eyes turned soft with sympathy. "Sorry about your grandmother."

"Thank you," she whispered, trying not to think about how alone she felt now that she lost her grandmother.

Raised in this small Colorado town after her parents died tragically in Kansas when a tornado ripped through their neighborhood, she adored the woman who took her in and loved her with her whole heart and always made her feel safe and never alone. Home again, she felt out of place. Old friends felt like strangers after so many years.

"How are things at the grocery store and ranch?" he asked.

"I'm making repairs and upgrades. Grandma left some things undone over the last couple years. I should have come back more often."

"Too busy building your career after college, I guess."

"You get lost in work, the days go by, and before you know it, years have passed. Look at you. I come back and you're a husband and father of two, all grown up."

"It happens. What about you? Did you get married?"

"Not even close," she admitted, thinking again about Grant, and what they'd shared. It had never been anything more than a one-night stand. For him. The ache in her chest swelled. No, she'd never found anyone who made her feel like he did, which is why every guy came and went in her life like they walked through a revolving door.

"Well, judging by the buzz around town, everyone knows you're back, even if you have been keeping to yourself. I'm sure you won't spend too many nights home alone."

"Nothing wrong with a quiet evening, especially when you work as much as I do."

"I heard you kept your job and set up an office in the grocery store. I don't know how you do it. Two full-time jobs, plus fixing up your grandmother's place."

"I've got good people working the store, and I enjoy fixing up the house and property. It's not so bad."

"Judging by the car you've been racing around town in, you must be doing pretty well for yourself."

Embarrassed, she only smiled. She loved the Porsche. The one splurge she allowed herself when success finally came at the end of several years of struggling to make the business profitable.

"So, what is it you do?" he asked.

"I work for a marketing company doing graphic arts. Computer programming. Stuff like that."

Seth gave her another of his famous smiles. "Stuff like that, huh? I heard you own half that business and it's booming."

"We do okay."

In college, her roommate majored in marketing. She'd majored in computer graphics design and programming. They started their own website, making advertising materials for small businesses. Soon, the business grew and they hired a few employees. Now, they had twenty-seven staff members, plus her and Carrie. Taylor could work anywhere, especially since Carrie kept the office running like a machine. She missed her friend these last few weeks and hoped to make a trip back to Denver soon. Once things settled down here in Fallbrook, she'd commute back and forth as needed, maybe spending a couple days a week in Denver. She'd have to find someone to take care of the horses at the ranch before she could even think about leaving for an extended period of time.

Again, she thought of Grant. Neighbors, in any other

circumstance, she'd simply ask him to take care of the horses in her absence. Not in this case. She couldn't face him. Obviously, they weren't meant to share anything more than one night together. He'd made that clear when he refused to speak to her about it, sent her on her way, and literally mounted up, turned his back on her, and rode away.

"You always were a quiet one. Maybe that's why we always got along so well. You never ran your mouth a mile a minute like all the other girls."

"Mommy talks all the time."

Seth rolled his eyes. "Yes, she does."

"Things are good for you. You've got the two girls, and I hear you're still working at the family ranch."

"Grant runs the place. I'm just the hired help."

Seth made it sound like a joke, but Taylor understood. Grant had always been the serious one, looking after his younger brother and the ranch when their father left them and their mother in the middle of the night. Grant became the man of the house at fourteen and took his responsibilities seriously. When their father left, chasing dreams and a younger skirt, the ranch had been in financial ruin, but somehow Grant turned things around.

Town gossip confirmed the ranch was prospering. From what she'd seen every day when she drove past the large spread, he'd certainly made something out of next to nothing.

"Oh, come on. You and Grant were always close. I can't imagine that's changed."

"He wasn't happy when I married Amy. He brooded

about it for months. I know things between you and me—"

"Ended because you wanted something better. Something right," she said and placed her hand on his arm. His smile softened when he looked at her.

"Not better. Well, yes, better," he added on second thought. "But that doesn't mean that what we had didn't matter."

"Let's chalk it up to rose-colored glasses. In the moment, we thought we had something. When we both looked more closely, we realized we wanted something else. We were young and having fun."

"No hard feelings?"

"None. Friends?" she asked, hoping to put an end to the past, this awkwardness between them, and move on to the future.

"Friends," he confirmed. "We always were, even if I messed things up for a while."

The door to the diner opened and Amy walked out with a cup holder in one hand and her daughter's hand in the other. She still looked beautiful. The girls shared their father's smile and hazel eyes, but they had their mother's creamy skin and dark hair. Seth stood just at six feet. Judging by the girls' long legs, they'd top their mother's five-foot-six frame in the coming years.

Amy didn't smile. Instead, her eyes narrowed, and she turned to the man walking out the door behind her. They exchanged a few words and for the first time in years, Grant locked eyes with her. The initial burst of shock on his face quickly turned to a deep frown, and he glared.

"I'm so happy we had this chance to talk," she told Seth, hoping to make a graceful exit before Grant and Amy closed the short distance between them. "I'm heading out. Maggie, I'm so pleased to meet you."

"Stay," Seth encouraged. "We're headed over to the park for the annual children's winter play. They're doing *Rumpelstiltskin*."

"Thanks, but I can't. I'll see you soon."

Unwilling to face Grant standing in the middle of the sidewalk with Seth and his family, she leaned up and gave Seth a kiss on the cheek and a smile before she turned and tried not to appear to be rushing away in shame and humiliation.

Grant had made it clear years ago she didn't belong anywhere near the Devane family. She didn't want to hear it again. Still, she wondered why he'd been so adamant about making her go away.

Chapter Two

GRANT STOPPED SHORT of running into Amy on the way out of the diner. He held tight to his coffee, afraid he'd spill it on her or Millie.

"What the hell is she doing with my husband?"

Grant followed Amy's line of sight and spotted his brother with Maggie atop his shoulders, and the woman who'd haunted his dreams, both waking and in sleep.

"Taylor."

He didn't realize he said her name until Amy turned her heated gaze on him. "Do something. It's bad enough he talks about her all the time. I won't let her sweep in and turn him away from me."

Like you turned Seth away from Taylor all those years ago.

Grant held his tongue because what he'd done after wasn't much better. Still, he'd paid dearly for giving in to his need for Taylor by letting her go. She didn't know that. He'd made sure she didn't know it. To this day, he still called himself a jackass every time he looked in the mirror.

Amy and Seth had hit a bad patch these last few months. The strain in their relationship hadn't quite eased, even with all the holiday cheer. The last thing they needed in the middle of their marital slump was a beautiful redhead with a smile that could fell a man at twenty paces.

Amy nudged him in the gut. "Get rid of her."

The last thing Grant wanted to do is make her go away. Then she stood on tiptoe and kissed Seth on the cheek, gave him one of those soft smiles that tied Grant in knots, and turned to leave on her own.

Grant's feet moved faster than his brain and carried him forward. Luckily, his mind started working when he caught up with Taylor.

"What do you think you're doing?"

"Going home," she answered without turning to look at him. Forced to stare at the back of her, his gaze settled on her gorgeous ass. He lost track of why he followed her for a second—or two.

"Grant, man, come on. The play starts in fifteen minutes. We need to get a decent seat so the girls can see," Seth called from ten steps behind him.

"In a minute. I have something to say to Taylor."

At the sound of her name, she stopped beside her car, and her head fell. She stared at the ground and waited for him to speak. For the life of him, he didn't know what to say. All the things he wanted to say got dammed up in his throat.

She probably wouldn't want to hear them anyway.

Without a word, her head came up. She unlocked her car door, opened it, but didn't get in. Instead, she stood behind it, making it a shield between them. He hated that she thought she needed the barrier. It also made him smile, because nothing would keep him away from her if she gave him even the slightest hint she still belonged to him.

So far, nothing registered on her face or in her eyes. She'd locked herself away from him. He needed to find the key. That one small thing that would tell him how to proceed.

"Well, what did you want to say?" she prompted, an almost imperceptible tremble in her voice.

"What are you doing here?"

"I live here," she defended herself, though he didn't know why she felt the need.

"I mean, what are you doing with Seth?"

"I ran into him."

"He's married and has two children."

"Yes, I know. Your nieces are beautiful."

"He married Amy because he loves *her*."

"I certainly don't need the reminder."

He hated putting that hurt look on her face, but she masked it well. The remark hurt her tender heart and that wasn't his intention. He hurt her once, but that was one too many times in his book.

"It's just that he and Amy are having some trouble

right now. They've just started to get back on track. They don't need you interfering."

"Here I thought saying hello, how's the family, was just good manners."

"Taylor."

"Grant."

He sighed and said without thinking, "Hello. How's the family?"

"They're all dead. Thanks for asking."

The woman turned his heart to mush and shut off his brain and revved up another part of his anatomy. Ever since she came home, he couldn't sleep, work, eat, anything without thinking about her. With her standing in front of him, he didn't know if he should kiss her or tell her to leave, before she killed him with wanting or ruined his brother's marriage.

"I'm . . ."

Sorry died on his lips when Seth clamped his hand on his shoulder and turned him around.

"Let her go, man. Everything is fine. We made up."

"What the hell does that mean?" His anger flashed. If Seth thought for one minute he could make up with Taylor and build a life with her, he had another think coming. Grant would see him in a grave before he let him leave his wife and family to marry Taylor.

"Dude, relax. We worked things out. She forgives me for what happened."

"Seth," Taylor called. "Really nice to see you again. We'll catch up later."

Grant turned and caught the glare she sent him. It may

have been nice for her to see Seth, but not him. No, he'd made a jackass out of himself when all he really wanted to do is talk to her—and take her to bed. God, did she have to look that good in her white sweater and black leggings? His mouth watered just thinking about how well the sweater hugged her curves. Her reddish-blonde hair hung well past her shoulders. He remembered the softness of it against his skin.

"Good-bye."

He hated hearing her say that word the last time. It irritated him even more now, because she made it sound just as final.

The slam of the car door definitely ended this botched reunion. He'd spent the last three weeks trying to figure out a way to approach her. He'd flubbed it up, big-time.

"Real nice, man. What is with you? You've always had some strange dislike for her."

No, he liked her. He loved her.

"What did she ever do to you?" Seth asked.

She turned my world upside down and left me alone in my misery.

"You need to get yourself a woman." Seth slapped him on the back. "It might improve your sour mood."

"I already have someone."

Well, maybe not yet, but he aimed to fix what he broke, and soon. Because no matter his good intention years ago, he couldn't live without her anymore.

"Who is the mystery woman?"

"Drop it," Grant warned. He didn't want to get into his relationship, or lack thereof, with Seth in the middle of the street with half the town scattered about them. Grant didn't want to tell Seth he slept with the girl he dumped for Amy. Seth may not have wanted Taylor, but they were brothers, and he'd crossed a line.

"Is that what you do with all those twenties you put in your jar? Hookers and strippers are not a relationship."

Grant smacked Seth on the chest and gave him a light-hearted shove. "Shut up. It's not like that, and you know it."

"I know you spend too much time working and not enough time living. You're four years older than me, yet I'm the one with the wife and kids. Don't you want that, too?"

The girls rushed them. Maggie went straight for Seth, and he scooped her up and plopped her on his shoulders again. Grant grabbed Millie and did the same. They walked as a family toward the park. Seth backed off and spoke softly with Amy, knowing Grant wouldn't say anything more until he was ready.

Grant thought of Taylor, home alone while the whole town gathered for the play. He wanted to go and be with her, but he needed time to think of the perfect way to approach her and make her understand what really happened all those years ago.

He adjusted Seth's oldest on his shoulders, and she giggled when he tickled her. How did he get the heavier load? Well, he'd been carrying the brunt of the weight all their lives. Maybe it was time he had more than a prospering ranch to show for it.

What would it be like to hold his own green-eyed, red-headed daughter or son in his arms?

First, he'd have to get Taylor back into them.

Chapter Three

GRANT STOOD HALF hidden behind a stack of detergent boxes in the middle of Taylor's grocery store with a basket in his hand, staring at her working in her office. She looked tired with her hair twisted and clipped up at the back of her head, tendrils of red and gold fire escaping here and there to trail along her face and shoulders. She slumped in her seat in front of her computer, and then pulled herself up straight and rolled her head from side to side, working out the kinks. He'd like to slide his hands over her shoulders, rubbing out her sore, stiff muscles, and kiss his way up her throat and take her sweet mouth, devouring her with one of those kisses they shared only in his dreams these days.

"You should tell her how you feel," a voice whispered in his ear from behind.

Startled, he turned and found Taylor's best friend from

high school. He ran into Rain all the time, but avoided asking her about Taylor, despite the fact she sometimes dropped information about her, like exploding M-80s, just before they parted ways. They'd exchange innocuous pleasantries, then bang: "By the way, Taylor opened her own business in Denver." So close, but still too far away.

He thought Rain knew what happened between him and Taylor, but never asked. He appreciated the bits of information she gave him too much to jeopardize receiving it by saying something stupid.

"I'm sorry, what?"

Ignoring his intentional misunderstanding, she went on. "You've wasted enough time. Too much time. Tell her how you feel. You've waited all these years. Did it not occur to you she's waiting for you?"

"You don't know what you're talking about." Maybe she did. He hoped that maybe she'd talked to Taylor about him and knew what Taylor really wanted.

He didn't want to admit to anything without knowing for sure.

"You wait and she waits and nothing happens. Make it happen," Rain coaxed.

"Mom," Rain's daughter, Dawn, called, walking down the aisle with her sister Autumn beside her. Both girls held boxes of cereal to their chests, arms wrapped around their prizes.

"Girls, you remember my friend, Grant."

"You played baseball with Dad," Dawn said.

"I sure did, honey. He was the best."

Everyone in town knew Brody and Rain's story. How

they fell in love, Brody made a stupid mistake, and left Rain, never knowing about his girls, and how Rain ended up with Autumn, Brody's daughter by another woman.

Grant gave Rain a look that said, "Haven't heard from Brody, huh?"

She barely shook her head, but the sadness in her eyes told him how much she wished she could say yes. If for no other reason than to tell Brody about his beautiful daughters.

"Will I see you at the Valentine's Sweetheart Dance in a couple of weeks?" she asked.

"Only if you promise me a dance," he said.

"You're on," she said.

He smiled but looked down at the girls. "I meant you two."

They beamed at him, though Autumn's smile was much more shy than her bolder sister's. "Yes," they both squealed.

"It's almost spring. I can't wait to see you two out on the field, playing softball with Seth's Millie and your uncle Owen again."

"We can't wait to see Mom pitch again."

"Rain sure does have a wicked arm," he confirmed, remembering seeing her play in high school when he used to hang out with Owen and Brody, though those two got into far more trouble than he ever did, being stuck on his ranch most of the time.

Rain followed his gaze to Taylor, even though he hadn't meant to give himself away by looking at her.

"We'll see you soon," Rain said, drawing the girls

away and walking straight for Taylor's office. The two women embraced. Taylor's gaze found his and her hand came up in a kind of wave, but then she stood back from Rain, smiling and exclaiming about how big the girls had gotten, and the moment passed.

Maybe he should make her dinner. She didn't look like she'd been getting much sleep, or any decent food, judging by the can of soda and bag of tortilla chips on her desk. He could call the store and ask if she'd bring him a gallon of milk on her way home. He'd surprise her, and they'd have a chance to talk in private and clear the air.

He wished he had the confidence that simply telling Taylor how he felt would set everything right and bring her back into his life for good.

"I'M SO SORRY about your grandmother."

Taylor embraced her dear friend and held tight, needing the comfort. Work and running the store did nothing to ease her grief, or the growing sense of loneliness.

In that moment, her gaze found Grant, staring at her from the cleaning-supplies aisle. She waved before thinking better of it.

"Thank you, Rain. I've meant to find you at home or at your father's garage to say hello." She'd purposefully kept to herself since returning home, giving herself time to grieve before she faced her old friends. Taylor stood back and stared down at the two beautiful girls. "They get bigger every time I see them."

"By the minute," Rain confirmed.

"Is Owen still in town, helping you out with the girls?"

"You'll see him at the Valentine's Sweetheart Dance."

"I will?"

"Yes, you will. You can't hide away on the ranch and in this office forever, you know."

"I'm not sure . . ." She hadn't even considered going. As a business owner in the community, she should probably attend.

"Nonsense. You can't spend every minute of the day working. You need to have some fun. I do love what you've done with the store. The new beauty counter is awesome."

They stared out Taylor's office door to the new makeup counter she'd created. Several young girls sat sorting through all the new products she'd ordered. The skincare specialist she'd hired from the local cosmetology school helped the girls pick out eye shadow colors and taught them how to do their makeup. It was a huge hit.

"We used to dream of having something so fancy in town when we were in high school."

Rain smiled. "You begged your grandmother to do something like this for years when we were kids."

Taylor fell into past memories and lost herself for a moment. Rain's face swam in front of her. Tears gathered in Taylor's eyes and fell down her cheeks.

Rain pulled her close and hugged her, whispering, "Someone watches over you."

Taylor wiped her eyes and thought of her grandmother. "Thank you for reminding me." She glanced back to see if Grant still lingered in the store.

"Maybe he'll come back." Rain winked, letting her know she'd caught her staring at Grant.

The thought of Grant watching over her made her insides warm, but she didn't admit anything to Rain. Up until now, no man had made her want marriage and children and a shared life. She shook her head and ruthlessly tried to block thoughts of Grant and her together out of her mind. Never going to happen. He didn't want her.

"So, you will be at the dance," Rain said, making the decision for her. "See you soon." She put her hands to the girls' backs and ushered them out of her office to the checkout line.

Maybe Grant would ask her to dance, hold her in his arms, and tell her he'd made a terrible mistake.

You wish.

Chapter Four

WHAT AM I doing here?

Grant left a message at the store, asking if she'd drop off a gallon of milk on her way home—no matter what time, he'd added. How did he know she worked late most nights?

Why didn't he order grocery delivery like everyone else? That's why she started the service.

Okay, so she lived next door. Technically. Three acres of land separated them. A hell of a lot more than dirt and grass stood between them. So what was she doing sitting in her car outside his house?

She had to admit, the place looked good. Her favorite azaleas were planted along the front porch. Two giant hydrangea bushes flanked the stairs. Their spindly branches spiked up, bare this time of the season, but in the spring they'd be full and gorgeous. Purple poppy mallow lined the path. Grant had certainly made a few changes since she'd been gone. She had to admit, he'd chosen well. The rest of the spread looked well tended. The beautiful horses in the pastures stood as testament to Grant's love and devotion to them and this land.

He swore he'd make something out of the nothing his father left behind. He'd certainly done that, but more, he'd proven his father wrong. Grant wasn't nothing, but he'd had to do this to prove it to his father, and himself.

He'd made his success and so had she, in a different way. They weren't the same people they'd been so long ago. The kid Seth didn't want turned into a woman in Grant's strong arms, but she'd become so much more, living on her own and making her own way. Their good-bye hadn't been easy, but if she'd stayed, she'd have missed out on so much and been a different version of herself. She liked who she'd become, but always wondered in the back of her mind what she'd have been if she'd stayed with Grant.

She'd have planted desert four-o'clocks, too.

She stepped out of the car and scanned the property, spotting the plant along the side of one of the barns and smiled. It always amazed her how much she and Grant had in common, despite their four-year age difference. He'd been so easy to talk to, and then he'd shut her out. She'd always wondered why.

The wondering kept her up at night and alone.

The porch light came on just as the sun fell behind the mountains, casting a grayish-purple glow over the property. She'd made it just in time. She'd drop off the milk and be home before it got truly dark. She'd do the chores and feed the horses, then finish painting the kitchen and spare bathroom.

She walked the plant-lined path to the porch steps and pulled her sweater closer. The milk jug weighed down her right arm. About to knock, the door opened, and Grant stood smiling at her, looking better than any man should. His hazel eyes did a quick sweep from her feet to her head, leaving everything in between hot and needy.

"I wondered how long you'd sit in your car, staring at the house instead of coming inside."

"If you knew I was here, why didn't you come out and get this?" She held up the gallon of milk.

He took it. "Thanks. What do you think of the flowers?"

"They're beautiful. Most of them are my favorites."

"I remember." She gave him a suspicious look, which only made him smile. "Come in, and I'll get you some money."

"It's okay, really."

"You'll go bust in no time if you give away food for free."

"I don't think one gallon of milk will break the bank." Despite her words, she followed him through the living room to the kitchen. The smell of spaghetti and fresh-baked garlic bread filled the spacious and bright room. Her stomach grumbled.

"When's the last time you ate a decent meal?" Grant put the gallon of milk in the fridge, but not before she saw the other nearly full one beside it.

Suspicious, she watched him closely. He tried to come off casual, but the way he kept staring at her said something else entirely.

"I had a granola bar an hour ago."

"What did you plan for dinner, cereal out of the box?"

"Since you don't actually need that gallon of milk, I can take it with me and have it with my cereal."

His eyes went wide. He let loose a nervous laugh and shook his head in self-mockery. "Busted."

"What is this all about?" she asked, her stomach tied in knots being this close to him again.

"I'm inviting you to stay for dinner."

"You could have asked me on the phone without dragging me out here with this ruse."

"You would have said no."

"You don't know that."

"I *dragged* you out here because I do know it."

He went to the sideboard and grabbed his wallet. He fished out five bucks and handed it to her. She stuffed it in her purse. He took a twenty, folded it in half and tossed it into the vintage two-gallon pickle jar nearly filled to the brim with nothing but twenties.

"You should put that in the bank. There must be ten grand in that jar."

"Over twelve thousand at this point."

"This place must make you a decent living. Why are you saving your money in a jar?"

"Every Saturday I put twenty bucks in the jar. That way, I never forget what I really want."

"What if someone steals it?"

"No one comes out here."

"What are you saving to buy?"

"It's not about saving. I can afford to buy the thing I want, but this is a way to make me remember sometimes doing the right thing can cost you everything, and maybe bring you everything you ever wanted."

"What? I don't understand."

"I hope soon you will."

"If this is about what happened between us—"

"This is about us. Period. Stay and have dinner with me. I owe you an apology for the other day."

Grant took a chance and reached out to cup her cheek in his hand. "I'm real sorry about your grandmother. I liked her a lot and miss seeing her at the store and at your place."

Her eyes immediately filled with tears, and she leaned into his palm. "I miss her every day."

With a swipe of his thumb over her smooth skin, he wiped away the single tear that fell from her lashes.

"Don't cry, sweetheart. You're going to be okay."

He hadn't realized he'd stepped so close to her until she planted her hand on his chest and pushed him away. Turning, she said, "I have to go."

He snagged her hand and held firm. "Stay. I made dinner. You're hungry." As if to prove it, her stomach grumbled. Loudly, making him laugh. "Give me a chance to make it up to you. I was an idiot yesterday."

"Only yesterday?" she asked, a grin brightening her face and sad eyes.

"We'll debate it over dinner. Come. Sit." He pulled her across the kitchen and into the adjoining dining room.

He'd left the lights off and a handful of candles burning on the table amidst the platter of spaghetti and meatballs, bread basket, and salad bowl. They cast a soft glow over the room and her surprised face. He kept his grip on her hand, so she wouldn't bolt, and used his other hand to grab the bundle of red roses lying on the table. He held them in front of her.

"Grant, what are you doing?"

"What I should have done a long time ago. I'm sorry for the way I handled things between us. I had no right, or cause, to hurt you the way I did."

"But you did have a reason."

"Smart and beautiful."

"Flattery won't get you out of answering."

"Not flattery. Truth. I owe you that and a lot more."

She took the seat he held out for her and waited for him to sit after serving her. He didn't speak, but stared at her until she took a bite. Her eyes fell closed as the first taste sent her into heaven. He was right. It had been a long time since she'd had a decent meal. She needed to take better care of herself.

"That's good."

"Having you here is better."

"Grant."

"I love the way you say my name." He poured her a glass of wine and smiled, happy this had gone better than he thought. She hadn't protested dinner with him. The way she kept looking at the roses told him she appreciated the gesture. Glad he stopped for them, he hoped everything else he'd done made her happy, too.

"The last time we spoke—"

"I made the worst mistake of my life. Eat," he ordered, hoping to keep her here long enough for him to explain and make her understand.

"You made it very clear you didn't want me anywhere near you ever again. Now you lure me out here under false pretenses, give me flowers, and make me dinner."

"No and yes."

"Excuse me." She picked up her wineglass and took a deep sip.

He made her nervous. The last thing he wanted her to be was nervous around him. Once, they'd been able to talk about anything. Then, she'd seen him as her boyfriend's brother. Not a man who wanted her. He never let her see that side of him, until one day he couldn't hide it anymore.

"I never said I didn't want you near me."

"You ordered me to leave."

"Those were my exact words. I didn't want you to stay here . . ."

"Right." She looked around the table and let her gaze fall on him. For the first time, he felt like she really looked at him. "So what the hell am I doing here now?"

She tossed her napkin on her half-eaten plate of food, scooted her chair back, and stood.

"Wait. Let me explain."

"You explained it well enough eight years ago and just now. I have to go. The horses need to be fed."

"I already fed them." He stood to go after her. She stopped in the dining room entry and turned back.

Again, her eyes scanned the intimate setting. "Candlelight, roses, dinner for two. Yesterday you demanded I stay away from Seth and his family. Today, this," she spread her hands wide to encompass the table. "Is that what happened all those years ago? You seduced me to keep me away from them, ordered me away to make sure I didn't interfere in their relationship?"

"Hell no."

"Right. One minute you want me in your bed and the next you want me out of town for good. I come back to town, you see me with Seth, order me to stay away from him again, and now you're trying to seduce me again. Why? Because you think I still have feelings for Seth?"

"Do you?"

"I'm not doing this with you again."

"Answer the damn question." The anger came with a swift kick in his heart. Everything had gone off track and taken a turn he never intended. After the way he'd treated her, he should have known she'd be suspicious of his motives. Maybe he'd laid the romance on a bit thick, but he'd wanted to do something nice for her.

"Funny, I thought I did when I slept with you. I thought that meant a hell of a lot more than any words we said to each other. You proved me wrong. It didn't mean anything more than the itch you scratched before you sent me on my way. Message received, then and now."

The front door slammed before his stunned brain started working again. "What the hell just happened?" he asked the empty room.

"Fuck."

He fell back into his chair. The house mocked him. He hated the deafening silence, and even more the intimate dinner he'd planned when he should have just talked to her, explained everything, and told her how he felt.

Like the dining room and kitchen, this was his mess to clean up. All he needed to do is figure out a way to make her want to listen.

Chapter Five

TAYLOR SLAMMED THE car door and stood in the middle of her yard, looking up at the star-studded sky, feeling like a complete fool, tears gathering in her eyes.

"I'm such an idiot."

She blinked, refusing to shed one more tear over him.

Instead, she sucked them back, swallowed hard, and went to the stables to check on the horses. She entered through the side door, flipped on the lights, and wanted to run out of here, just like she did Grant's house. The damn man left his impression everywhere he went. He'd left it on her, like he'd marked his territory. Every other man paled in comparison because she constantly measured them against a man who didn't want her. Not really. All he wanted to do is keep her away from Seth.

Ridiculous. She didn't have feelings for his brother. Didn't he see that? Hadn't she proved how much she loved him when they slept together? Apparently, her novice attempt to say without words how much she cared came off as nothing more than a pleasant distraction for him. An enjoyable means to an end.

She lifted the lid on the feed bin. Full to the brim. He'd dumped the heavy forty pound bag in, knowing she'd used up all her strength dragging the bag into the barn in the first place. He'd brought down several bales of hay from the loft and stacked them in an empty stall. Not only had he fed the horses, but all of their coats gleamed from a recent brushing. He'd mucked out all the stalls and fixed the broken water line in Star's stall. She gave the horse a rub up the neck to her ears. The scents of horses and hay mingled and calmed her. She loved the horses and wished she had more time to spend with them. She'd love a nice long ride.

On her way out, it hit her. The stables were much brighter than they'd been last night. She glanced up to the twenty-foot ceiling and hated the smile that spread across her face. He'd changed the bulbs on all four burned-out fixtures and cleaned the cobwebs.

She didn't want to, but she'd have to thank him.

He used to tease her about her fear of heights. He used to tease her about a lot of things back when she spent time at his house with Seth. Of course, he only ever spoke to her when they were alone.

She stopped short in the dark yard and thought back to that time in their lives. As often as she spent time at the Devane ranch to see Seth, do homework with him, or just hang out, Grant only talked to her in any meaningful way when they were alone. He'd send Seth on some errand or chore that couldn't wait, and then he'd stay with her. They'd talk like old friends. His interest had seemed genuine, if not tentative. Like he didn't want her to know he liked her. But he did like her, or at least she thought so at the time. She'd felt comfortable with him, drawn to him even. Her teenage hormones certainly went crazy whenever she saw him. Some days, he'd be out working in the hot sun, shirt off, sweat glistening on his sun-tanned skin. Funny, looking back, she didn't remember ever feeling that hot and bothered about Seth. In fact, most times she went to see him, she'd hoped to catch a few of those precious moments alone with Grant.

They'd felt like stolen moments.

Like tonight. The two of them alone in the dining room, candles and flowers and good food. She'd imagined being alone with him again. It should have been so perfect, but it wasn't because once upon a time he'd sent her away. She still had the broken heart to prove how much his rejection hurt.

She entered the house through the back door and sighed. The kitchen stood in ruins, everything stuffed into boxes, the cabinet doors taken off the hinges, propped against the frames and lying on the countertops. Well, she refused to dwell on Grant and his conflicting attitude. What possessed the man to do her chores, fix things in the barn, make her a beautiful dinner, only to continually warn her away from his brother?

She didn't know.

Was that what really happened?

"Stop thinking about it and do something," she ordered herself. Always better when she acted, she grabbed the roll of blue painter's tape, started at the back door, and worked her way around the room, blocking out thoughts of handsome men with hazel eyes who make amazing spaghetti.

She worked into the early-morning hours before she succumbed to exhaustion, only to dream of Grant making love to her on a bed of red rose petals. Even when she woke up, she could swear she smelled them. The scent of fresh-brewed coffee overlaid the heady sweet scent of flowers.

She rolled off the couch she'd collapsed on last night and walked to the kitchen, drawn by the smell and curiosity. She hadn't made the coffee, so who did?

"Grant."

His name filled the room, just like his presence, though he was long gone. She must have slept like the dead, because he'd cleaned up all the tape and paint-splattered paper she'd used to cover the floor and countertops while she painted the walls. He'd rehung the freshly painted cabinet doors with the new hinges she'd bought last week at the hardware store. The kitchen looked perfect. Warm and cheerful pale yellow walls contrasted with the crisp white cabinets. She poured a cup of hot coffee, walked to the table, and picked up the note lying next to the vase filled with the red roses he'd handed her last night—but she'd left behind.

I'm sorry.

Her gaze scanned the kitchen and landed on the covered pan on the stove. She walked over and pulled the lid off, revealing the still warm egg, cheese, and spinach omelet inside. He couldn't have left that long ago.

She sat at the table with her plated omelet and cup of hot coffee. Her gaze wandered out the window to the stables. The wheelbarrow sat outside, a shovel sticking out. Guess he'd taken care of the horses for her this morning, too.

Someone watches over you.

Rain's words. She looked at the eggs, the coffee, the wheelbarrow, and her kitchen. She remembered the new lightbulbs in the barn.

"Maybe so, but what does it mean?"

Chapter Six

GRANT RODE DUSTY into the stables and stopped him outside his stall door. Seth came up behind him and slapped him on the back.

"Is that an actual smile? Did you just get back from shacking up with some hot chick?"

Grant tried to wipe the smile from his face, but couldn't. He hoped Taylor appreciated all he'd done for her. He hoped she understood his *I'm sorry* note meant for everything. They still had a lot to talk about, but he wanted to give her time to settle down and think about last night and the past and see the truth. God, he hoped she finally understood what he'd been trying to tell her for too damn long. He was tired of waiting and living alone and missing her.

"Who's this mystery woman?" his brother asked.

"None of your damn business."

Grant pulled the saddle from Dusty's back and tossed it on the rack. He pulled the pad off next and grabbed a brush and worked it over Dusty's coat while he chomped on a piece of apple Seth handed him.

"Were you with Taylor?"

"No." Okay, maybe he'd said that too quickly and sharply. "Why would you ask me that?"

"Why won't you look at me?" Seth shot back.

Grant sucked it up, glanced over Dusty's back, and stared straight into his brother's eyes. He waited for Seth to make some crude comment or silly joke. He didn't and the serious look disturbed him.

"How long will you wait before you go after her? It's been eight years and four weeks and still you do nothing but work yourself to sleep every night."

Stunned, Grant didn't know what to say.

"I'm not the idiot you think I am. Okay, maybe I didn't totally figure it out until we saw her the other day, but I get it now. You want her. You wanted her back in the day. That's why you always found some random excuse to get her alone. I thought you were just being your usual ornery self, but that wasn't it at all, was it?"

Grant opened his mouth to spit out some random lie, or joke the subject away, but he couldn't bring himself to do it. "No."

"Did you two hook up all those times you sent me out to the stables to feed the horses, or finish some chore?"

"No. Nothing ever happened until I found her crying after she caught you cheating." He let the anger out with his words. He couldn't believe his brother would treat Taylor so poorly.

"Are you seriously mad I cheated on Taylor?"

"Why didn't you break up with her if you wanted to see Amy? You didn't have to hurt her like that."

"Things between Taylor and I weren't headed in that direction. We were friends, not lovers."

"Yeah, I found that out."

Grant wished he could take those words back.

Seth's eyes narrowed. "Did you sleep with her?"

"What happened between us is none of your business."

"You did," Seth accused. "You slept with her, and then sent her away. That's what she meant."

"What are you talking about?"

"After Amy and I got together, I went to talk with Taylor. Before I ever said anything, she broke down crying, saying she knew about Amy. She got the message, the Devanes didn't want her. I felt terrible, but she wasn't talking about me. She was talking about you. Her reaction to my being with Amy seemed over the top. We never shared any deep feelings for each other, not enough to make her that upset. You didn't want her. You hurt her far worse than I ever did."

"I took advantage of a young woman, angry and grieving over what you did. I thought she slept with me to get back at you."

"That is some fucked-up shit."

"Don't you think I know that? Don't you think I've

paid for it every day that she's been gone? Don't you see me still paying?"

"You're in love with her."

Grant didn't answer. He hadn't told her, he wasn't going to confess to Seth.

"You drove her away. Why?" Grant's continued silence didn't stop Seth from figuring it out. "It wasn't just that you thought she loved me. You pushed her away because you thought if you convinced her to stay with you, she'd leave you eventually, like Dad left. Mom loved this place like you did, but Dad wanted something different and better than how he'd grown up his whole life. You thought if you asked her to stay, eventually, she'd leave you for something better.

"Amy thinks you're some player, using women for days or a few weeks then dropping them without ever knowing anything more than their name and what they like for dinner."

"I don't really care what they want to eat," he admitted. Okay, so maybe he'd been a selfish bastard with women over the years.

"You didn't want any of them. Every one of them, nothing but a placeholder, because you want her," Seth spoke the unvarnished truth.

"Yes, damn it. I want her."

"What the hell are you waiting for? Go get her."

Grant leaned back against the stall door and let out a self-deprecating laugh. "You think it's that easy? You said it yourself, I hurt her."

"If you could hurt her, that means she cares."

It took her leaving more angry with him than she ever was with Seth for him to realize she cared for him deeply, and he'd screwed it all up.

"When the hell did you turn into some philosopher?"

"When I saw the way you looked at her the other day. It all clicked."

"Yeah, well now all she does is glare at me."

"You talked her into bed once before, do it again."

"What if I told you I want a hell of a lot more than her in my bed?"

"If I thought that's all you wanted, I'd be warning you not to mess with her again, instead of asking why you're still standing here."

Grant let out a frustrated laugh again and shook his head. "I'm regrouping. I blew it last night."

"Couldn't have been all that bad if you're riding home just after dawn."

"It's not what you think. I went over early this morning to leave her an apology gift."

"So you two—"

"Are still circling each other."

"She's interested?"

Grant had to think about it. Yeah, for a moment last night he'd seen the way her eyes roamed over him, and she'd remembered being in his arms and wanted him again. If only she'd forget he hurt her. Not going to happen, and completely up to him to make her forgive, if not forget.

"Let's just say, I have my work cut out for me."

"Maybe it's time you directed your single-minded determination from the ranch to her. That's what this has all been about. You made this place into somewhere she'd want to stay."

"You want to get out of my head. It's creepy when you read my mind."

"So, that's it. You did all this for her?"

"I started out just wanting to prove the old man wrong. This place didn't ruin his life—he ruined this place. I built it back up because it is a good place to live and work. It's a good place to raise a family and live a good and honest life."

"Yes, but you live here alone."

"I'm trying to fix that."

"You're not doing a very good job if you're leaving her apology gifts."

Grant frowned. "I'm out of practice with her. We used to talk to each other so easily."

"Yeah, while I shoveled shit."

"Literally," Grant said, smiling. More seriously, he asked, "Do you care that I want to be with her?"

"Do what makes you happy, man. She and I were friends. Even if we did flirt at more, it never turned into anything."

"Why does Amy think it was?"

"You thought it was. I don't know. Who can figure women out? I left Taylor for her. I married her. You'd think both those things would convince her I love her."

"When's the last time you told her that?"

Seth opened his mouth and clamped it shut again. Grant felt for him. It couldn't be easy to get married so young and start a family right away when you were still growing into being a man.

"By the time she cleans up after dinner and puts the girls to bed, it's all we can do to fall into bed together."

"Maybe you could get the girls to bed early for her. She might like it if you pitched in."

"I help out."

"You sit on the couch and watch TV."

"Now you sound like her."

"I'm just saying, if you gave her a break, she might give you one."

"You make up with your woman, and I'll make up with mine."

"Is it going to be weird for you and Amy if things between Taylor and I work out?"

"Not for me, man. I mean it. I hope you two are happy together."

To prove it, Seth put out his hand. Grant took it. "Who knows, maybe if you're sleeping with Taylor, my wife will finally believe I don't want to."

Grant laughed. "Anything I can do to help."

Seth laughed with him and Grant let go of his worry that he'd put a rift in their relationship. The last thing he wanted to do is gain Taylor in his life, only to lose his brother and family.

Chapter Seven

TAYLOR DRAPED THE garment bag over the passenger seat. She smiled, thinking of the new dress she'd bought for the Valentine's dance. She wanted to knock the socks off Grant. Show him what he gave up.

Oh, face it, you want him to want you.

She shook off those conflicting thoughts and slid behind the wheel. She kept her speed in check through town, but hit the back roads with a need for speed. She loved racing around the curves.

Despite being tired after another fourteen-hour day at the store, she found the drive energizing. She'd driven home several hours ago to tend the horses, secretly hoping to run into Grant, but he didn't show up. Why would he? He wasn't responsible for taking care of her animals. Still, she'd wanted to see him and clear the air. If she planned to stay in town, they couldn't keep dancing around their past. They needed to say their piece and be done with it.

Still, some part of her would always want him. Maybe she only wanted him because he didn't want her. You want what you can't have. Just like a stubborn child, she held on even when she should let go.

Disappointed, she'd gone back to the store, worked for a few more hours, stocked shelves for another hour, and finally given in to exhaustion to drive home. She pulled into her driveway and parked, noting she must have left the light on in the kitchen. She grabbed her dress and headed inside, stopping short in the entry. She stared at the covered dish on the counter and the piece of paper propped against it with the words, *Eat something*.

Tears filled her eyes when she pulled the cover off. Steam rose off the thick slice of meatloaf with mashed potatoes with gravy and green beans.

"How does he know when I wake up and get home?" She grabbed a fork from the drawer and took a bite. "Damn, the man can cook." She stood in the middle of her kitchen, her purse still hanging from her shoulder, and devoured the plate of food. Like most days, she'd barely eaten. Finished, she finally tossed her purse on the counter and washed the plate in the sink.

Damn, I really need to thank him now.

A smile spread across her face. She'd been missing her grandmother and thinking about all the little things she enjoyed about her. Most of her memories were of baking right here in this kitchen. She turned to grab one of the boxes she'd packed up when she repainted the cabinets and discovered all the boxes missing from the dining area. She opened one cupboard, and then the next, and discovered all the dishes stacked and neatly put away on the new cork shelf liner she'd bought and Grant must have installed.

"He must spend half his day here. I need to start locking the door."

What good would it do? He knew the key was under the miniature pink rose pot on the back porch. Besides, he probably had a spare key, since her grandmother had often asked him to look after the place when she visited her in Denver.

Well, he'd done several nice things for her; the neighborly thing to do was thank him properly. He may not like her, but he wanted to leave the past behind, fine. She could do that. All the nice things he'd done for her didn't mean he'd changed his mind about her. They lived in a small town. They couldn't avoid each other forever, but they could be cordial.

She grabbed the butter from the fridge, the flour from the pantry, and gathered all the other ingredients she'd need to make her grandmother's famous peach cobbler.

Grant's favorite.

Chapter Eight

GRANT ROLLED OVER and punched his pillow. The alarm signaled the end of another bad night of sleep and a morning waking up alone and wanting. He shifted uncomfortably, his hard cock rubbing into the mattress. All he wanted to do was bury himself deep into Taylor's soft warmth. He groaned and rolled onto his back, bringing the pillow over his face, and holding it there to muffle his frustrated growl.

He'd forgotten to make the coffee last night and set the timer.

"Great. No Taylor and no coffee. Another fucking great morning."

He rolled out of bed, grabbed his sweatpants, and dragged them on. Half asleep and irritable as hell, he walked into the kitchen, and stopped midstride. The scent of fresh brewed coffee hit him first, then the delicious peach cobbler. He gazed out the window at the dark sky, the sun not yet ready to make its appearance, or even cast a soft glow to back off the night.

"Doesn't she ever sleep?"

He grabbed a mug and poured the coffee. The note he'd left her last night—*Eat something*—lay propped against the covered dish he'd brought her. Filled to nearly overflowing with his favorite peach cobbler. He did what he'd told her to do. He plated up a huge helping, sat at the table, drank his coffee, and ate the sinful concoction.

"Damn, the woman bakes even better than her grand-mother."

Stuffed and caffeinated, he put his plate in the dish-washer, the cobbler in the fridge, poured another cup of coffee, and took it up with him to the shower. He had a lot to do today.

Showered, shaved, dressed, chores done, he stopped by Taylor's place to be sure she'd fed the horses before she left for work before dawn. He headed into town himself near noon for lunch before he stopped off at the feed store and picked up a new leather bridle for Taylor's horse. Since she'd been home, she hadn't gone riding once.

With school out for the day, Seth promised the girls they'd go to the park and play softball. Practice for the up-coming season. He spotted Seth's truck and pulled in next to it. He got out to find his brother and the girls, thinking of playing ball with his and Taylor's kids one day.

"You're a long way off from that yet."

"A long way off from what?" Amy asked, coming up behind him.

"Nothing. Just thinking out loud. Where are Seth and the girls?" he asked, not seeing them in the park.

"Over there."

Amy pointed across the street to the shops, but neither of them moved when they spotted Seth with Taylor, together on the sidewalk. She smiled up at Seth, and he leaned down and gave her a peck on the cheek. Grant's gut burned with jealousy, but he checked his first impulse to kick his brother's ass. *It's nothing. They're friends*, he reminded himself.

"Why can't she stay away from him?" Amy asked.

"She's just saying hello." He defended her because he knew deep down that's all it was. Right? She couldn't possibly still have feelings for Seth. They grew up together. Maybe at one time they'd thought a few hormonally induced kisses meant something more. Obviously, it hadn't amounted to much if Seth ended things to be with Amy.

"You might remember Seth married you. He loves you. He and Taylor have been friends since they were toddlers."

"They dated in high school."

"They hung out together. If you're honest with yourself, you'll remember they didn't have anything as combustive as you and Seth when the two of you got together."

"Well, things have fizzled."

"All it takes is a spark to start a flame."

"Seth mentioned there may be a spark between you and Taylor."

"She thinks I hate her."

"Do you?"

"Not even close."

Amy smiled, and her eyes danced with delight. "You two would be great together."

"You mean, better me than Seth."

"No," she said quickly. "I mean it." Her head cocked to the side, and she stared at Taylor. "She suits you. You're both . . . driven. You both come from complicated families. She lost her parents. You lost your father. It may not be the same, but you'd both understand each other's loss and wishing for something different."

"I want to make something different with her," Grant admitted, testing the waters to see if Amy objected to Taylor in his life and a part of their family. The last thing he wanted to do is alienate Amy, or spend every birthday and holiday at some tense family meal that no one enjoyed or wanted.

"I didn't know you two knew each other that well."

"We did once."

Amy gave him a knowing smile. He kept his face blank. He'd given enough away already. He didn't want to play his hand before he'd been dealt all the cards. He still needed to have a real conversation with Taylor and somehow win her back.

"Let's go say hello." Amy took the lead, walking straight to Seth and wrapping her arm around his waist. She leaned up and gave him a kiss. Seth smiled down at her, a touch of surprise in his eyes. "Taylor, it's so nice to see you again. How are you?" Amy asked.

Seth's eyes went wide. Amy gave Grant a look that told him she really liked the idea of him and Taylor together.

One worry eased, a dozen more to address with Taylor once he had her alone.

Taylor banked her shock and answered Amy as friendly as she'd been. "I'm fine. How are you?"

"I'm great. I love this time of year. The bright sun, cold, crisp days, don't you?"

"Yeah," Taylor said, stamping down the lonely feeling welling up inside of her. Cold nights spent alone. No family. Her friends all back in Denver.

She must not have concealed her feelings well enough, Grant's eyes softened on her with sympathy as if he'd read her mind.

"Taylor," he said by way of greeting.

"Grant."

"Thanks for breakfast."

"Thanks for dinner," she said, letting her gaze fall from his.

"Did you two . . ."

"No," they answered Seth's unfinished question in unison.

"It's between us," Grant added, meeting her gaze and giving her a serious look she didn't understand at all. Why did he always make her feel off balance?

Did he have to look that good in tight jeans and a heavy black coat hugging his broad chest? He looked warm. She wanted to slide the zipper down, wrap her arms around him, and hold tight and soak up some of his heat. She should have added a scarf to her outfit this morning. And put on her heavier jacket.

The girls wandered across the street to race around the trees in a game of chase, squealing and laughing.

"Well, nice to see all of you. I need to get those boxes to the store." She pointed to the stack of boxes outside Eli's Auto Repair.

"What is all of that?" Grant asked.

"I've heard of a few families in need this winter. Rain and I had an idea to do a secret admirer gift exchange at the Valentine's dance. We ordered things for women, men, and children at different price points. People can buy a gift, or make a donation in their sweetheart's name. I'll use the proceeds to deliver meals and help pay heating bills."

"That's a wonderful idea. I'll stop by later and buy a couple of presents and make a donation." Amy beamed her a smile, making Taylor even more confused.

Maybe Seth finally convinced Amy she didn't have designs on her husband. Well, the change of heart made things easier, especially since they'd inevitably run into each other at the store and in town.

"I found these really cute Valentine's clothespins that I thought people could use to pin their donations to the huge heart-shaped quilt Rain put together." The red-and-white blanket lay folded on top of the boxes.

"That's a wonderful idea. I'll help spread the word to all the kids' moms at Maggie and Millie's school."

"Thank you." Uncomfortable with Amy's unexpected help, her voice came out too soft, making them all stare at her even more. "Enjoy your afternoon." She made a hasty retreat and walked down the block to Eli's to finalize the plans with Rain.

Grant stared after her, but addressed Amy. "Thanks."

"You're welcome. Go after her."

"You know?" Seth asked.

Without really answering, she said, "I know she's your friend, and I have no reason to dislike her."

They shared a kiss so filled with emotion, Grant looked away, feeling like an intruder on their moment.

Grant left them to their family outing, mustered up his gumption, and trailed after Taylor down the street, searching for a redheaded goddess with a golden heart. Donations for families. He'd never met another woman with such a kind heart. Except maybe her grandmother, who Taylor must miss terribly right now.

Eli stood outside the bay door next to a Ford truck, talking with a customer about a tire rotation, but turned to him when he entered. "Hey, Grant, can I help you?"

"I'm looking for Taylor."

Eli's dark brow went up along with half his mouth in a knowing smirk. "She's in back with Rain."

She stood in the office doorway, her shoulder braced against the door frame. She had both hands around her middle to ward off the crisp chill in the air. He pulled off his coat and draped it over her back and shoulders, startling her. He didn't miss the way she turned her head and smelled his jacket. Her eyes half closed, she caught herself and took a hasty step back, but she tugged the jacket closer betraying how she really felt.

"Hey, Rain," he said to his friend sitting at the desk.

"Hey, yourself. Looking good, cowboy."

"Thanks. How are the girls?"

"Great. Can I help you with anything?" she asked, her gaze going from him to Taylor and back.

"I'm here for her," he confirmed. He turned his focus back to Taylor. "I thought you might need some help with those boxes out front."

"Um, I can manage. Thanks."

"No way you fit even one of those boxes into your tiny Porsche. I've got the truck parked down the street at the park. Come on, we'll get it loaded up and over to the store."

"Grant, you don't need to help me. Rain is busy here today, but I thought to ask Owen to do it with his truck."

"You don't need someone else. You have me."

"Why are you doing all of this?"

All, meaning the chores at her place and the two dinners. He wanted to tell her, but he didn't want this to be a public conversation. Rain, Eli, the two other customers that came into the garage all witness to every word they said. Every look that passed between them. The nervous looks Taylor cast about said she didn't want to do this here either.

"You know I don't do anything I don't want to do." He gave her a second to let that settle into her stubborn mind. If she'd just look at him and see what was right in front of her and believe it, this would go a whole lot easier. Hell, nothing had ever been easy in his life, why did he expect getting the woman he wanted to be any different?

"Lead the way, sweetheart."

He held out his arm to get her to go ahead of him back

through the garage bay. Her gaze fastened on his arm and chest and all he wanted to do was grab her. He sucked in a breath to try to calm his revving engine and took a step toward her. Unfortunately, she turned and walked ahead of him, giving him a nice view of her gorgeous ass. He tried not to make it obvious he'd follow her anywhere, but Eli's grin told him he hadn't quite pulled it off.

They stepped outside together. She pulled his coat tighter around her.

"You need to wear warmer clothes, sweetheart. You'll catch your death. Winter holds on this time of year."

"I got sidetracked this morning and forgot my warmer coat."

"I know just how you feel. I've gotten sidetracked a lot lately."

She frowned again, so he changed the subject. "Let me pull the truck up. I'll get these boxes loaded. We're losing daylight. I have things to do." For her. If his hard body was any indication, he'd never make it more than a few more days before he had to have her or die a miserable death. They had to clear the air. He'd have to get her alone and talk to her.

She waited for him to get his truck and lift the heavy boxes into the bed. Her eyes never left him. He felt her gaze touch every part of him, making him that much more in sweet agony for her. It also told him how much she wanted him, even if she wasn't quite ready to see he needed her in the same way.

"I'll follow you to the store and help you get this set up."

"You don't have to. One of the guys can help."

"I want to." Their gazes met and held, and he hoped she finally got it. The confusion in her lovely green eyes remained even when she turned and headed for her car, parked a few spaces down. She slid behind the wheel and stole another glance at him. He smiled and felt lighter, despite the confusion still on her face.

It didn't take long to set up the display at the store with the heart-shaped quilt hanging on the wall by the front doors, the decorated clothespins outlining the blanket. He had to admit, it looked good.

"Where's the sign you made requesting donations?"

They'd worked in silence together. He couldn't say it felt comfortable, but they'd relaxed into it. Seemed they were both waiting for something to happen. He only hoped she waited for the same thing he wanted. Them to finally be together.

Taylor propped the sign on the floor at the bottom of the quilt. She set another sign on the table where she'd set up pink boxes with white hearts on them for people to put in their requests for secret-admirer gifts. She put out a pretty wrapped present with a special card she'd made with a Valentine's wish to go with the gift.

Taylor stood back and admired their work. Not bad at all. She especially liked doing it with Grant, even though she'd never admit it to him. She didn't understand his need to help her, but she appreciated it.

He moved in behind her, his heat radiating against her back. Close, he asked, "You made the signs?"

"This morning. You like them?" She stared at the caricature of a family standing together.

"It's perfect. Can you be home by six tonight? I want to show you something."

"Yeah, I guess."

"Great. I'll see you later." He placed his hand on her head, his fingers gently pulling her hair into his palm. His voice came out deep and husky at her ear. "You know, that mom and dad remind me of us."

Her gaze fell to the picture of a family again and she gasped when she realized, in a way, she had in fact drawn a perfect representation of them.

"You're a wonderful artist. See you tonight." He gave her hair a soft tug and kissed her on the side of the head and left her standing there staring at the picture, making excuses in her mind for using their images without ever thinking about it.

"Hey, I came to see the display. It looks great." Taylor didn't respond. "He's right, you know. That looks very much like the two of you," Rain said from behind her.

Unable to take her eyes from the sign, she spoke without thinking. "Do you think it could ever be real?"

"Only if you make it real," Rain said, placing her hand on her shoulder. "Your heart knows what it wants, the only question is will you allow yourself to believe in him enough to make it a reality?"

"Can I believe in him?"

"Your heart already does. Follow it and it will lead you right to him."

Tears ran down her face.

"He pushed you away once not because he didn't want you, but because of his own insecurities and hang-ups. He's paid for that mistake. You both have. Now, he wants to give you everything."

Taylor stood there so long, she didn't know Rain left her to ponder the impossible.

When the tears dried, she focused on the display again and realized several of the clips held five-, ten-, and twenty-dollar bills. Grant not only helped her get set up, he'd started off the donations.

Old Mr. Green from the hardware store stepped up beside her, fishing a five from his wallet. He clipped it to the heart and gave her a pat on the shoulder. "Your grandma would have thought this a great idea. Before you know it, this will be filled. Are you attending the dance with anyone?"

She didn't have an answer to the simple question. Grant's face popped into her mind and a dozen dreams of them spending the evening—every evening—together. Nothing more than Rain's words invoking wishes. Only one way to find out if Rain was right. Could it be as simple as believing he cared for her and wanted to be with her? Is that why he'd gone out of his way to help her out the last few days?

Was she really this stubborn?

Yes, her grandmother's voice echoed in her mind, making her smile.

"Please excuse me, Mr. Green. I have somewhere I need to be."

Chapter Nine

TAYLOR DROVE INTO the yard. Her horse, Star, stood saddled and tethered to the fence. A bright yellow sticky note on the saddle horn. She walked over, gave Star a pat, and read the note.

Come ride.

Star nickered and another horse answered. She looked up and found Grant on his own horse, waiting at their property line. He looked so good in his black Stetson, the coat she'd snuggled into earlier, his tight jeans, and black boots planted in the stirrups. He sat atop the huge sorrel with confidence, all the time in the world to wait for her to join him because he knew she would. She couldn't fight it anymore. She didn't know why she'd tried.

She held up two fingers to indicate she needed a few minutes. He tipped his hat to let her know he'd wait. Something inside told her he'd wait all night if that's what it took. She stared a moment longer, letting that thought take hold. He'd waited. He'd wait even longer. He'd keep waiting until she was ready.

Grant leaned forward in the saddle, rested his forearm on the horn, and stared intently back at her.

"That's right, sweetheart, I'm not going anywhere without you."

Grant hoped with everything inside of him she'd finally realized that, or at least something close.

She ran for the house, and he held his breath waiting for her to come back out. When she did, he liked what he saw. Faded jeans, a heavy shearling jacket to keep her warm, boots on, hair tied back in a ponytail. She mounted up and rode toward him at a trot.

"Let's go."

"You order me around with very few words. 'Eat something.' 'Come ride.'" She held up his note. "'Let's go.'"

"You don't seem to mind," he pointed out, nervous about finally being alone with her. Especially after how badly the last time went.

"Where are we going?"

"You'll see."

He reined his mount around and trotted off to the left, Taylor following. He gave her a minute to settle in the saddle, then increased his mount's speed. They galloped over the land and up into the hills. He steered her through a small copse of trees. They emerged on a rise overlooking his land and hers, the sun setting in the distance casting a soft yellow-pink glow to the sky and land.

"This is beautiful," she said, sitting beside him, their

horses so close together, their legs rubbed against each other.

He wanted to drag her from her horse and onto his lap and kiss her. "I love it up here."

"Me too, except your place looks a lot better than mine. I've still got a lot of work ahead of me to get the ranch back in shape. It'll have to wait until spring."

"Does that mean you're staying?" He'd wanted to ask her for so long, but dreaded hearing the answer if it was no.

"The town needs the store."

"Anyone can run the store for you. You didn't answer the question."

She never looked at him, just stared over the land and watched the sunset.

"I've missed this place, my grandmother, the people."

"Anyone in particular?"

"More than I'd like to admit."

Her softly spoken words sent a shaft of relief through him so profound he slumped in the saddle. He reached out and took her hand and brought it to his lips. Her gaze found his when his lips touched her soft skin. He kept his lips there until she settled and relaxed. With her hand in his, he rested both on his thigh. They watched the sun fall from the sky and the stars twinkle to life.

Dusk cast a gray glow to the landscape. "We should get back before it gets too dark to see," he said, releasing her hand and turning his mount to lead her home.

He wanted to take her to his place, but decided better of it.

He dismounted outside the barn and walked to her. Before she did or said anything, he grabbed her by the waist and lifted her off her mount to the ground in front of him. Her hands lingered on his arms. They stood together in the yard, staring at each other.

"Go inside. I'll take care of the horses and be there in a minute. We need to talk."

He expected a refusal, or some kind of balking, but she gave his arms a soft squeeze, released him, and went to the back door without a word.

He tried to calm his nerves, working over both horses with a brush and finishing off the chores in the barn. Nothing worked.

Ready to face their past, he walked toward his future, determined to make her listen this time. Hopeful she felt the same way he did.

Chapter Ten

GRANT FOUND HER standing in the living room, staring at the photograph he left for her on the mantel among her family photos. His mother had taken the picture without their knowing. He found it in the house a few years ago after his mother packed up and moved to be with her sister in Arizona. The picture showed them alone at the pasture fence. She sat atop the rail. He stood next to her with his arms braced on top of the fence next to her legs. She stared down at him with a bright smile on her face. He looked up at her, smiling, something he'd rarely done back then, and usually only with her. His mother had captured perfectly the bond they'd shared, the connection between them, and the love they'd both had in their eyes when they looked at each other.

He'd stolen one of the Valentine's cards from the display she put up at the store—a pink heart with the words

Be Mine in red—and propped it up against the antique silver frame.

"Another demand?" she asked, her voice soft and timid. So much so, she made his heart ache.

"Not this time. A simple request."

She touched her fingers to the frame. "It's beautiful."

"You're beautiful."

Unable to help himself, the words fell from his lips. The crystal lamp on the table nearby cast her in a soft ethereal glow that highlighted her red hair and pale complexion against the deep green sweater hugging her body and hinting at the cleavage he desperately wanted to touch and taste.

"Why are you doing all this now, when you worked so hard to make me believe you hated me so long ago?"

"I never hated you. Don't you see what I see in that picture? I . . ." The word *love* stuck in his throat. He'd never said it to anyone. She'd been the only woman who'd ever invoked any strong emotion in him. He desperately wanted her, and his feelings gnawed at him every time he saw her, nudging him to do something to keep her with him forever. "I like you."

"No you don't. You can barely stand to be near me."

That's because I want to rip off your clothes every time I see you. "You just got back. We've barely had a chance to say hello. When we did, you weren't exactly happy to see me."

"Forgive me if my hello didn't seem warm and genuine. You were warning me away from your brother for absolutely no reason."

"You try to come off cold and indifferent to me, but once we were hot together," he reminded her.

"Maybe, but the frostbite I got from you afterward hurt like hell."

"I'm sorry." The words sounded flat, when he meant to put a world of meaning behind them to prove to her he truly meant it.

"Have you ever said you're sorry to anyone in your life?"

"No. That's how much I like you." He smiled, liking that even when they didn't see eye to eye, they could still find the humor in things. "I am truly, deeply sorry I hurt you."

"You like me," she said, a touch of disbelief in the words, hiding the trace of hope he heard, and hoped he didn't make up for his own sanity.

"I *like* you," he repeated.

"Is this some kind of joke?"

Maybe he couldn't say it, but he could sure as hell show her. He grabbed her by the back of her neck and pulled her close. Surprised by his abrupt touch, she gasped a second before he took possession of her mouth. He slid his tongue deep and tasted her for the first time since they made love. God, his dreams didn't do justice to actually having her close. She smelled like heaven, tasted like sin, and made him want to break every rule and be the best man he could be all at the same time.

Just like their first time, she exploded in his arms, giving back everything he gave to her. She slipped her tongue into his mouth and moaned when his tangled with hers. Her small hands fisted in his shirt at his sides and she pulled him close. Plastered to his front, she rubbed her breasts against his chest when she rose up on her toes to take the kiss deeper.

This time he groaned and slid his hands around her hips and cupped her bottom, tilting her hips against his. He ground his hard cock against her, and she rolled her hips against him.

Before things went too far, she tore her mouth from his and pressed her head against his shoulder, panting as hard as he did for air.

Without looking at him, she asked, "You *like* me?"

"I'm trying to show you that I do."

She sucked in another shuddering breath and boldly asked, "Are the middle two letters in that word wrong?"

It didn't take him more than a second to figure out what she asked. Sliding his hands from her pretty bottom, he held her hips firm and coaxed, "Look up."

Her head came up and her apprehensive gaze found his. She gave him a lopsided smile at his two-word order.

"Yes. The letters in that word are wrong. I've never said it to anyone who wasn't family, so I'm working my way up to saying it right. After what happened between us before, proving it to you seems more important at the moment."

"I still don't know what I did wrong."

"Nothing," he said, his tone emphatic. The last thing he wanted her to think was that she'd said or done something to turn him away, when all he'd wanted to do is hold on.

"Maybe you should explain what happened."

"You were there. I thought I taught you well, but if you need another lesson"—he pressed his thick, aching cock to her belly—"I'm happy to oblige."

She pushed him away. He gave her some space, because he needed to cool off before he dragged her to the braided rug and had his way with her.

"If all this is about getting me back into your bed, then forget it. Been there, done that, hated the parting gift."

His head fell. He stared at his boots for a second. Damn, she wanted to talk. A real explanation. He closed the distance and stood behind her, his hands clamped onto her shoulders so she couldn't get away.

"After we made love, you were lying in my arms, your head on my chest and over my heart, and all I could think was that somehow you'd claimed the damn thing. You didn't just have sex with me, you put everything in you into it and that somehow made me put everything into it. You didn't know to hold yourself back from giving a piece of yourself, but I did, and with you I didn't care. You made me want to give you everything, anything to keep that feeling we created together. I've never felt closer to anyone in my life. I wanted to hold on to it, and you, and never let go."

"You did let go."

"I thought I was just a poor substitute for the man you really wanted. If you'd stayed, I feared that what I did would damage my relationship with Seth, his relationship with Amy, and my tenuous relationship with you. I deserved it for taking advantage of you."

"You didn't take advantage of me. I wanted you."

"I know that now." Frustrated, he raked his hand over his head. "I only wish I'd realized it sooner. Everything in me wanted to convince you to stay, but you deserved better than what little I'd managed to scrape together at that point in my life. I had nothing to offer you and a hell of lot to take away. Look at what you've become, sweetheart. A college graduate, business owner, brilliant artist, and so much more. I couldn't ask you to stay here and give all that up."

"So you cut yourself off from me without a word of explanation. I didn't care what Seth and Amy did. I wanted to be with you."

"You wanted to go and learn and live your life and grab hold of all those opportunities in front of you. I couldn't take that away from you. My life is tied to my ranch. You needed to decide that you wanted to come back here on your terms. No regrets you missed out on something, or gave it up to be with me."

"It has to be all or nothing?"

"Yes. Isn't what we feel for each other worth that? I don't want pieces of you. I want all of you. I want you every day and all the time. Forever."

"For a man who can't say one four-letter word, you sure do have a way with other words."

He turned her to face him, cupped her beautiful face in his hands, and stared into her bright green eyes. "I love you." Her eyes softened and a huge smile bloomed on her already kiss-swollen lips. "Enough talking."

He bent, grabbed her by the bottom, and brought her

up in his arms. She wrapped her legs around his waist, and he took her mouth in a kiss so filled with passion and heat, he nearly fell to his knees right there in the living room and took her on the floor. Instead, he kept his head and carried her to the bedroom.

He set her on her feet at the end of the bed and stared down at her upturned face, waiting for his kiss.

"If you don't want this, me, and everything that comes next, say so now, otherwise, you're mine."

"Love me."

"Ordering me around?"

"It works for you."

It sure as hell did, and he didn't waste time proving he'd forever be at her beck and call, especially when she was in his arms.

He yanked off his boots first. She tore his shirt over his head. Happy to oblige her wandering hands and roving mouth, he stood before her, playing with her long silky hair while she pressed openmouthed kisses to his neck and down his chest. He grabbed the hem of her sweater and pulled it up and off. She gave him a shy smile when he traced his fingers down her shoulders and chest to roam over the swell of her breasts. He used his index fingers to push the bra straps off her shoulders and bent and kissed her breast above the satin cup. She sighed and he pulled the barrier away, licked her hard nipple, and took her into his mouth, softly suckling. He reached around her back and undid the clasp, tossing the bra away, so he could touch and taste both breasts to his heart's content.

Her fingers worked their way through his hair. She

held him to her, and he gave himself over to pleasing her, touching every soft plane and curve of her body and soft skin. He leaned her back until she fell onto the cream-colored spread. She shimmied back, giving him the perfect opportunity to strip off her jeans and panties. He pulled off her boots along with her clothes.

He stared down at her, naked and laid out below him, and felt so damn lucky and happy and starved for her. "God, you're beautiful. I need you so damn bad."

"Show me."

Another order he complied with, smiling. He stripped off the last of his clothes, tossing his jeans over a chair, but not before he grabbed the condom out of his pocket and tossed it onto the pillow at the top of the bed. He leaned over, planting his hands on either side of her. She sucked in a breath, the first sign of hesitation, but she quickly relaxed when he kissed his way up her thigh to her hip. Their gazes met, he leaned up, and settled between her thighs.

His lips met hers with an urgency he turned to soft demand when she opened for him, and he stroked his tongue into her mouth, and her soft, sweet hands roamed down his back and up again. Tentative at first, those first few touches became steadier, more assured as they learned each other all over again. Like the first time, he discovered the soft hollow at the base of her neck and licked it with a hot sweep of his tongue, making her sigh. He kissed a trail down her neck and chest to her breast, swept his tongue across the rounded underside and up to her puckered nipple, begging for his mouth. He clamped his lips over the tight bud, suckled hard, and made her moan.

Her legs clamped around his waist, and she pulled him close, his hard cock pressed against her cleft. He rubbed forward and rocked back.

"Grant."

He loved his name on her breathless sigh.

"Not yet."

He needed her wanting him as much as he wanted her. He mapped her belly with his tongue and lips, nipping and kissing his way down to heaven. Her honey-sweet taste on his tongue, he drove her to the peak, but didn't let her fall. Instead, he slid up her body and took her mouth. Her hands rubbed up his chest and over his shoulders, up his neck. She reached above her and grabbed the condom, unwrapped it, and sheathed him.

Overwhelmed with the need to bury himself deep in her warmth and love, he needed something from her infinitely more. He needed her to believe in him.

He pressed his forehead to hers and looked her right in the eye. "I love you."

She must have seen the need in his eyes, because she gave him the answer he desperately needed to hear.

"I know you do."

In that moment, he let himself go and put everything he had into making love to her. He left no part of her untouched or unloved. He devoted himself to making up for lost time. She didn't disappoint either. For every stroke of his hand, sweep of his tongue, give and take of his body to hers, she gave everything back to him with equal ferocity or tenderness as the pace changed, shifted, built to a crescendo years in the making.

Sated, well loved, Taylor lay on his chest, her head over his thrashing heart, and whispered, "I love you, too."

He kissed her on the top of the head and gave her pretty bottom a squeeze. "I know you do. Now you believe I do."

"What now?" she asked.

"You'll see."

Chapter Eleven

TAYLOR STOOD IN front of the mantel, staring at the photograph of her and Grant with her hand over her nervous stomach. Grant's car rumbled to a stop outside, but she didn't move. He'd come find her, kiss her on the temple, then on the lips, like he did every night. Tonight, however, they weren't staying in for dinner and making love into the wee hours of the night. No, tonight they'd drive over to the community center and attend the Valentine's Sweetheart Dance, despite the fact that Valentine's actually fell on Monday, tomorrow. She couldn't wait to see her good friend, Rain, but worried what people would think of her showing up with Grant. No one had known about them back in the day, and their being together now might seem sudden. Maybe they were taking things too fast?

"Stop thinking," his deep voice rumbled at her ear a

second before he kissed her on the head, turned her, and said, "Better yet, I'll make you."

He kissed her then and all her worries disappeared, replaced with thoughts of Grant and her and the wonderful times they'd shared over the last two weeks.

Grant ended the kiss with a few soft nibbles at her lips and raised his head just enough to meet her gaze. "You're so beautiful." She smiled and he relaxed beneath her hands. "There's the smile I didn't see a minute ago."

"You're gorgeous."

He smiled and held her in his light embrace. "You just figured that out."

She smacked him on the arm, then smoothed her hands over the white dress shirt covering his rock hard chest. She gave herself over to the pleasure of touching him.

"Did you tell Seth we're coming together?"

"If you keep touching me like that, we will be in just a few minutes. I promise."

Her cheeks flamed, but she laughed anyway, knowing he tried to make her relax.

"Sorry. I can't help myself."

She pulled away, but he held her close.

"If tonight wasn't important, I'd have you stripped to the skin, and riding me all night. But I hate to muss you up when you look so damn good in that dress."

Midnight blue, the pretty fabric sparkled in the light. She'd fallen in love with it the moment she'd seen it. She'd secretly hoped he'd see her in it, but never dreamed he'd be her date to the party.

"Why did you say tonight is important?"

"All our friends will be there. People have seen us in town together, and they're talking. Tonight, everyone will know we're together. They'll see we love each other."

"Does it matter what everyone thinks?" she asked.

"I only care what you think. What's really bothering you?"

"No one knows about our being together before. When they see us now, they might think it's kind of fast."

"Honey, I waited eight years for you to come home to me. I'm not slowing things down because of someone else's sensibilities. Anyone who can't see how much I love you and want to be with you is blind. If they judge us for being happy, then that's their problem.

"Unless you're the one who wants to slow things down," he added.

She read the hurt and fear in his eyes. So easy to read him now that they'd spent so much time together talking, catching up on their lives, sharing their meals, and practically living together day after day. No, it hadn't been long, but they'd both waited too long to find the happiness they both felt when they were together.

"I think things are perfect between us."

He kissed her hard and deep, his relief evident in the overwhelming need he showed her. He broke the kiss and traced his finger over her jaw. "We're perfect together."

"I just hope your family feels the same. Seth and Amy will be there tonight."

"Don't worry about them. They already know about us, and both of them are wildly happy for us."

"They are?"

"Yes, they are. Let's go."

He grabbed her hand and drew her with him out of the house to his waiting car. She stopped short and stared at the nearly new Mercedes.

"I've only ever seen you in your truck."

"I bought this about six months ago in case I needed it."

"For what?"

"Driving a pretty woman on a date."

She crossed her arms under her breasts and glared at him. "What pretty women?"

"I said, a pretty woman. You. Your grandmother told me you were planning on moving back to help her with the store."

His hand swept down her hair to her shoulder, because she hadn't made it back in time before her grandmother passed.

"You've been planning my coming home for six months?" she asked.

"I've been planning since the day you left."

"Yeah, right."

"You'll see," he said, and helped her into the silver car.

Chapter Twelve

THEY ENTERED THE large barn, transformed into a country ballroom, complete with beautiful refurbished crystal chandeliers, strung white lights, and masses of white, pink, and red flowers with trailing ivy greenery. The rustic place sparkled and seemed enchanted. The historical society had transformed the old place and made it a unique country community center where people held meetings, parties, and weddings year round. The white linen-draped tables had heart-shaped confetti in pastel colors. In the center of each table stood Styrofoam hearts with sayings on them, like *Be Mine*, *Kiss Me*, and *You're Cute*. Just like the sweet tart candies every kid received when they passed out Valentine's cards at school.

"I haven't been here since they started work on restoring it. It's beautiful."

"Yeah. I've been here often for birthdays, weddings,

and holiday parties. You missed the Christmas party." When she frowned, thinking of her grandmother, he squeezed her hand. "I hoped you'd come, but understood it was too soon for you."

She didn't answer, but didn't need to—he understood her heart.

Grant pointed across the way. "There's Owen. I haven't seen him since our last kickboxing match at the gym. We like to see who can kick whose ass at least once a week. So far, we're even."

She stared up at him in disbelief.

"Don't worry. You'll know everything about me soon enough. Besides, I had to work off all the energy I stored up, waiting for you to come home to me."

She smiled and socked him in the gut. "Town gossip says you didn't work out some of that energy only in the gym."

"Doesn't mean I wasn't still waiting for you. It took you a damn long time to come home."

She believed him and the jealousy disappeared as fast as it swept through her. He meant it and because he did, she settled even more easily into loving him.

"Every time I come to one of these functions, I watch the guys with their wives and think how empty my life has been without you. Now, you're here with me, and I'm so damn happy."

"I'm glad you feel that way. Now, you'll get to introduce me as your girlfriend."

"Tonight's the first and last time I intend to introduce you as that."

"What do you mean?"

"You'll see."

Grant dragged her into the crowd before she had too much time to think about what he'd insinuated. He headed straight for Owen, standing with another man she hadn't seen since high school.

"Owen, nice to see you, man." Grant shook hands with his good friend, but kept Taylor's secure in his other. "Dylan, home visiting your parents?"

"No. He's the new sheriff," Owen announced with a slap to Dylan's back.

"No kidding. When did that happen?" he asked.

"If you left that ranch of yours more often, you'd know he took over when Sheriff Leland retired a week ago."

Dylan gave him a knowing smile. "I see why you've stayed home. Taylor, so nice to see you again. How long's it been?"

"Wipe that grin off your face, man. She's my girl-friend." Yep, that description lacked the depth of his feel-ings and relationship with this woman. His buddies must have realized it, too, because they both gave him a look.

Taylor moved them back to the subject. "Last I saw you, we were in high school."

Dylan's face took on a far off-look, his eyes so filled with regret and sadness she hated reminding him of that time. She'd heard the rumors about the girl he took to prom. Jessie? She disappeared a few days after he gradu-ated. Town gossip said her father killed her.

Owen changed the subject. "I'm real sorry about your grandma."

"Thanks. I miss her."

"The whole town does," Owen said. "She was a fixture. Last time I saw you, you were off to college. I thought you'd be smart enough by now not to hook up with the likes of this guy."

"Oh, well, he's not so bad."

Grant gave her a smile and said, "Thanks, honey. A glowing endorsement."

"No endorsement needed. I know you're a great catch."

He smiled down at her and kissed her in front of his friends and practically the whole town. No doubt the show of affection didn't go unnoticed.

"Oh, look, there's Rain. I'm going to say hello. You boys have fun." Taylor walked away to meet up with Rain and her girls.

Grant watched her progress and forgot all about the two men watching him.

"So, when's the bachelor party?" Owen asked, slapping him on the back.

"If it were tomorrow, it'd still be too damn far away for my liking," Grant acknowledged and took the glass of beer Dylan handed him.

"She's more beautiful than I remember," Owen said.

"Didn't she used to date your brother?" Dylan asked.

"For all of five minutes," Grant snapped.

"All I have to say is it's about time you found a wife and settled down. Stop letting your little brother show you up with a wife and kids and happy life while you're turning into a grumpy hermit," Owen teased.

Grant laughed, finally took his eyes off the woman

across the room and faced his friends with a smile on his face. "I haven't been alone in weeks."

The guys raised their glasses, gave him knowing smiles, and saluted him. They drank, caught up on old times and new, and settled into the evening with off-color jokes and lighthearted bantering.

Chapter Thirteen

TAYLOR LEFT GRANT to his buddies and steered her way through the other guests, greeting those she knew until she reached her friend.

Rain's dress sparkled under the lights when she moved forward and hugged her. "You made it. I see you didn't come alone either."

Taylor followed her friend's gaze across the room and found Grant still staring at her. She smiled and he smiled back, making her insides melt.

"How are things going between you two?" Rain asked, handing her a glass of champagne.

"Great. Better than great," she admitted. "We talked and cleared the air. If I'd known he wanted me all those years ago, I might have stayed."

"You are who you are now because you left. He is who he is now because you left. You are both who you should be, so you can be together and make it last," Rain said, making complete sense. At least to her.

Taylor put her hand on Rain's arm and gave it a squeeze. "I hope Brody comes back."

"He won't," Rain said, a flash of pain marring her eyes.

"Trying to convince me, or yourself, you actually believe that?" Taylor asked.

"Just trying to do my best to raise those girls without giving them, or myself, false hope."

Taylor felt for her friend. She understood the kind of hurt and pain Rain felt, losing a chance at love. Time. Distance. Nothing would change the way she felt about Grant. Maybe one day, Rain would find that again and next time it would last forever.

"Come, let's go mingle with the men," Rain suggested when Taylor's gaze roamed back to Grant.

They joined the men. Grant never let her far from his reach, keeping one arm around her waist, his big hand planted on her hip. Other times, he held her hand, his fingers twined with hers. Maybe things between her and Grant were new, but they were based on years of knowing each other as kids and teens, and as lovers—long ago, and now.

Seth, Amy, and the girls joined them at their table for dinner, along with Owen, Dylan, and Rain and her girls. The atmosphere remained fun and festive and Taylor settled into the night.

Soft music played after the meal. Owen grabbed Rain's hand and pulled her up. "Come on, save me from dancing with . . . anyone else but you," he said, eyeing the women seated at the next table, hoping one of the most eligible bachelors in town turned his eye their way.

Dylan followed suit and took Dawn's hand, helping his son Will to follow along with Autumn to the dance floor for some fun. They all looked so adorable dancing together—Dylan on his knees in front of Dawn, Autumn holding on to Will's hands and swinging them from side to side.

Grant brought Taylor's hand to his lips and kissed it softly, like he'd done so many times in the last weeks.

"Let's dance."

Without a word, she stood and followed him toward the other dancers and walked straight into his arms. She held him close and let the music move them.

"Having fun, sweetheart?"

"Yes. This place is amazing." She loved the lights and flowers and the feeling. Most of all, she loved being around these people. They felt like friends and family.

"I used to dread coming here."

"Why?"

"Seeing all the happy couples, I'd miss you more."

"That's really sweet."

"It's the truth."

"Look at the children with Dylan. They're having so much fun."

"Do you want to have children?"

"Of course. Don't you?"

"Yes. Absolutely. Soon," he added, but she didn't respond. "Did you ever order a new mattress?" he asked, changing the subject, still holding her close and swaying to the music.

"I haven't had the time."

"I'm getting you a new bed. That old mattress you keep making me sleep on is killing your back and mine. Mostly mine, since you sleep on top of me."

"Which you love."

"Still, you need a new bed." He didn't tell her the new bed was in his house, in his room. She'd find out soon enough. That's if he pulled this off.

"Let's go home. It's late. Even the children are yawning." He pointed to little Will, whose eyes were drooping as he wrapped his arms around Dylan's leg.

"You just can't wait to get me back into bed," she teased.

"You know me so well."

They found Seth and Amy in the crowd and said good-bye.

On their way to the door, they stopped to say good-bye to Rain, Owen, Dylan, and the children.

"Oh, you're leaving?" Rain asked, standing by the table of Valentine's gifts they'd put together for tonight for all who'd bought one at her store, or donated money.

They exchanged a long hug. "Don't forget your gift." Rain handed her a white wrapped box with a red ribbon.

"But . . . who bought me a Valentine's gift?" she asked surprised and taken off guard.

"I did." Grant squeezed her hand.

"But it's not one from the store."

"No. This one is from me. You can open it on the way home."

"Grant, I don't know what to say."

"You say it every time you tell me you love me."

"Oh God, we've lost him to the dark side," Owen grumbled, rolling his eyes at Dylan.

"He's a goner for sure," Dylan added.

Rain punched both of them in the arms. "Knock it off." She turned back to Taylor. "Are you working at the store tomorrow?"

"She'll be with me," Grant answered for her.

"I will?"

"Yes. We have plans."

"Sounds like you have plans to tell me about," Taylor said.

"You'll see."

"You keep saying that."

"It's true."

Taylor shook her head and hugged Rain again. "I'll see you soon. The girls looked beautiful in their pink party dresses."

"You should have one," Rain coaxed.

"I'm thinking about it," Taylor admitted, feeling Grant's gaze burn into her back. He didn't say no way, or balk in any way, so she let the idea take root and waited to see if it grew.

Owen slapped Grant on the back, bringing him back to reality. "Looks like you've got some work to do tonight. Enjoy," Owen said to both of them by way of good-bye, making Rain smack him on the arm and laugh.

Grant dragged her to his car, started the engine, and drove out of the parking lot.

"Can I open my gift?"

"Not yet."

They drove out of town. He held her hand and they settled into the quiet, content to let the night settle around them, and enjoyed the ride. She held the box on her lap, anxious to open it, but loving the anticipation all the same. He'd done so many nice things for her, but he'd never actually bought her a gift.

Her house flew by on the right, and he drove on to his place. She didn't question him, despite the fact they always stayed at her place. He turned right into his long driveway and gave her hand a squeeze.

"Now, you can open it."

She pulled the pretty red ribbon free and unwrapped the box. She opened the lid and stared at the key inside on a heart shaped key ring.

"Is this the key to your heart?"

"Yes," he answered without cracking a smile. "And our front door."

He stopped the car in the driveway, the headlights spotlighting the porch and front door.

"Stay with me."

She'd wanted to hear those words from him years ago when he'd told her to go. This time she could honestly say she had no reservations. This is where she wanted to stay. She wanted to be with him. Here. "Always."

She didn't realize she spoke the last out loud, until he hauled her out of her seat and across his lap and his mouth settled over hers for a long, deep kiss. She didn't know how he managed to get them both out of the car in that tight space, but he did. With her hand in his, he pulled her along the path to the front door. He stopped long enough for her to use her key to let them inside. The smile and look in his eyes told her how much he loved it and her.

He guided her through the dark house and into their bedroom, stripping her of every stitch of clothes on the way down the hall before making love to her like his life depended on it. He did let her sleep on top of him, his arms banded around her the whole night.

Chapter Fourteen

TAYLOR WOKE UP with a jolt when a big, cold hand clamped on to her thigh. She wanted to pull away, but as always, Grant pulled her close and wrapped her in his arms. She snuggled close and sighed, shivering as her body warmed his.

"Good morning, sweetheart."

"Mmm, morning. Why am I hugging a popsicle?"

"It's cold outside."

"You should have stayed in bed with me."

"I have a surprise for you."

She opened her eyes, disoriented for a moment. Grant's bedroom, not hers. She'd slept so well last night, she'd forgotten where she was. She had to admit, he had a point about her bed. It sucked. The laugh bubbled up from her gut and she smiled. He'd promised her a new bed. Apparently, he'd delivered. In a sneaky sort of way, but she didn't mind.

"What are you laughing about?"

"You got me a new bed."

The look on his face changed. He smiled, but his eyes held a hint of uncertainty and nerves.

"I hope you'll use it every day."

She snuggled into the soft mattress and him. "There's no place I'd rather be."

Her admission changed something in him again and he rolled her under him and stared down at her, his gaze intense. "I hope you mean that."

His lips met hers in a soft, lingering kiss that melted her heart and made her want to give everything. It didn't take long for his big body to heat against hers and his hands to slide over her body in a blazing trail that set her nerves on fire. He made love to her with an intense, quiet passion. She'd never felt more loved and cherished in her whole life. She didn't know what prompted his need to show her this kind of heartfelt attention, but she responded, pouring her love for him into every touch and kiss and press of her body to his.

She lay spent, draped across his chest, her head resting on his shoulder, and her face tucked into the side of his face and neck. He rubbed his chin against her cheek and whispered, "Happy Valentine's Day."

The smile bloomed on her face when he squeezed her tight and kissed her on the nose.

"Come riding with me. There's something I want to show you."

She propped her chin on his shoulder, content to stay right here in bed with him the rest of the day. "Is this part of your plan to spend the day together?"

"It includes breakfast."

"I'm in." She scrambled from the bed to beat him into the shower, but he stopped her at the door, calling her name.

"Taylor."

She turned back. "Yeah."

"I love you." He lay sprawled in their rumpled bed, looking adorably handsome and well loved with his tousled hair, bare chest above the white sheet covering the rest of him, his head resting on his arm behind his head. That same intense look in his eyes drew her back to him. She planted her hands on the bed, leaned down, and pressed her lips to his and held the kiss for a long minute, their eyes locked. She ended the kiss and hovered over him, an inch away, her gaze never leaving his.

"I love you."

They met in the yard an hour later. Grant stood beside their saddled horses, looking nervous. He didn't speak, just helped her into the saddle, his hand resting on her thigh when she sat waiting for him to get his horse. He didn't move, just looked up at her and gave her a soft smile.

"You're so beautiful." He reached up and tugged her heavy coat together at her chest to make sure she'd stay warm. His fingers brushed over her hair.

She didn't understand his quiet mood, but she appreciated his attention and returned it, raking her fingers through his hair and trailing them down the side of his face to cup his jaw.

"You are one gorgeous, sweet man." She smiled down at him, leaned in, and kissed him.

Ready to ride, Grant took the lead and kept the pace brisk, but not too fast. He needed time to calm his nerves. He really hoped she liked this surprise. He'd thought about this moment for so long. He wanted everything to be perfect.

They stopped short of their destination and dismounted.

"We aren't riding up to the rise that overlooks the properties?"

"Do you trust me?"

"Of course."

"Close your eyes." She did without hesitation, making his heart soar. She trusted him completely. No questions. She simply believed in him and did what he asked.

He took the bandana out of his coat pocket and tied it around her head and eyes so she couldn't peek.

"Where's the trust?" she teased, making him smile and easing some of his tension.

"Trust me. This will be worth it." He hoped those words came true. Everything he was and wanted in this life depended on the outcome of the next few minutes.

He led her up to the rise to the exact spot he'd picked out.

"Don't move."

He left her for a moment to grab what he needed and came back to stand in front of her, blocking her view of the gorgeous land spread out below them.

She sensed his presence and reached out to grab hold of him by the shoulders.

"What are you doing?"

"Take the blindfold off."

She shook out her hair and blinked several times, focusing on him and the pickle jar filled with red, white, pink, and silver hearts he held in his arms. Confused, she stared from him back to the jar.

"You finally deposited your money in the bank."

"I invested it. Open your gift."

She unscrewed the lid and put her hand inside, pulling out the red heart-shaped card with the string attached. A diamond solitaire hung from the end, spinning, the diamond sparkling in the bright sunlight, a red bow keeping it in place.

"I invested in you."

He bent on one knee and set the jar to the side, taking her free hand. Her breath came out in wisps of fog in the cold morning air, her eyes locked on a spot just over his head.

Taylor gasped. Below them, on the point where their land met, he'd used stones to form a heart with two simple words inside.

Marry me.

Another two-word order Taylor swore she'd comply with as soon as possible.

Taylor hoped so much for this to happen one day soon. Overwhelmed with joy and so much love for this man, she let the happy tears fall from her eyes.

Taylor still held the ring in her fingers. Grant took her hand and held it and the ring between them.

"I have been waiting for you my whole life. Please, Taylor, do me the honor of becoming my wife. Live here with me. Build a life with me. Raise a family with me. I'll love you every day for the rest of your life and mine. Will you marry me?"

"Yes." The word burst from her lips and she covered her mouth with her hand and waited for Grant to untie the ring and slip it onto her finger. Still on bended knee, he stared up at her with a huge smile on his face. He launched himself up to his feet, grabbing her around the waist and hauling her up against his body and spinning her around. She slid down his chest and he kissed her, pouring all his love and happiness into the moment. She couldn't help it, she smiled against his lips, then laughed when the joy inside of her burst free.

He led her over to the picnic blanket he'd set out and pulled her down to sit next to him.

"When did you do all this?" she asked, brushing her fingers over the thick red plaid blanket and marveling at the basket filled with muffins, a hot covered dish filled with egg, cheese, and bacon scramble, and a bottle of orange juice and champagne.

"Right before I woke you up. I hope the eggs are still hot. That cover thing is supposed to keep the casserole dish hot for up to two hours."

"You're an amazing man," she said, accepting the mimosa he'd made for her.

"Took you long enough to figure that out," he teased, giving her a quick kiss.

Unable to stop herself, she laughed and clinked her

glass to his. He pulled her close and she sat between his legs and leaned against his chest, staring out across the land and the beautiful heart and message he'd built for her below.

"It's wonderful, Grant. I love it."

"I love you." He wrapped his arm over her chest and squeezed her into his body, keeping her warm on this frosty winter morning. She didn't mind the cold. Not when she had Grant and his love to keep her warm.

"When will you marry me?"

She wanted to spend the rest of her life with him. No doubts. No fears. Everything felt right.

"Very soon."

He hugged her and kissed her sweetly on the temple. "Good, because I'm done waiting for you." He kissed her again, long and deep and filled with love. She settled back into his chest and they held each other close, enjoying the morning and knowing their future was together. "We'll have a long and happy life together. You'll see."

She believed it.

A week later, he brought her back up to the rise for another surprise. He'd updated the heart-shaped message to read, *G.D. Loves T.L.*

The day after they returned from their honeymoon, on a bright summer morning, he brought her back to show her that *G.D. Loves T. D.*

When the tears came to her eyes, he whispered the sweetest words she'd ever heard in her ear: "I love you, Mrs. Devane."

Will Taylor's friend Rain find
her "happily ever after"?
Return to Fallbrook, Colorado,
to find out, in the first book in
New York Times bestselling author Jennifer Ryan's
The McBrides series

THE RETURN OF BRODY MCBRIDE
Book One: The McBrides

**Coming March 2014
from Avon Impulse**

About the Author

JENNIFER RYAN is the *New York Times* and *USA Today* bestselling author of The Hunted series. She writes romantic suspense and contemporary small-town romances featuring strong men and equally resilient women. Her stories are filled with love, friendship, and the "happily ever after" we all hope to find. Jennifer lives in the San Francisco Bay Area with her husband and three children. When she isn't writing a book, she's reading one.

Please visit her website at www.jennifer-ryan.com for information about upcoming releases.

Visit www.AuthorTracker.com for exclusive information on your favorite HarperCollins authors.

Sweet Fortune

Candis Terry

This one is for you, Amy Valentini, and your sweet heart.

Chapter One

For MOST PEOPLE it took a life-changing event to realize one needed to make changes.

For Sarah Randall, it started with a cookie.

Raised in a household erected on lectures of fire and brimstone and eternal damnation, Sarah had never been the type to take fortune cookies, fortune-tellers, or even *Wheel of Fortune* seriously. All that changed on a crisp autumn day in Los Angeles as she sat inside the Golden Chopstix Chinese Restaurant munching fried rice and Szechuan chicken.

Alone.

Again.

It didn't take an Einstein to realize something was severely lacking in her life. But it might take more than Cinderella's Fairy Godmother and "Bibbidi-Bobbidi-Boo" to figure out how to fix it.

She contemplated the upcoming Thanksgiving dinner she'd be expected to share with her oversized and always virtuous family. A gathering where those who shared her blood would pass the plate, as well as the conversation, around her without actually including her.

Avoidance of her current situation wasn't the answer.

As she sat in the restaurant's red vinyl booth, her mind reached back to what Charlotte—aka Charli—Brooks, her former boss on the TV makeover show *My New Town*, had once said. *"It's always good to experience new things."* Charli not only handed out good advice, she led by example. In the little town of Sweet, Texas, she'd found exactly what she'd been looking for and she'd gone after it. Or *him*, much to Reno Wilder's initial dismay.

Wedding bells were now in Charli's forecast, while Sarah's life was still on hold.

After Charli parted ways with the TV show, Sarah—much to Charli's dismay—became unemployed. She had thirty days remaining on the lease to her apartment. Her savings account dripped blood. And somehow, having fallen into the middle of the pack of eight children along with her extrovert sister, she'd allowed herself to become completely invisible.

Even her love life was on an IV drip.

The last time she'd been asked out had been on a blind date set up by a co-worker who'd been trying to pawn her brother off on someone. Anyone. Not that Sarah had a right to be choosy, but her date had made Sheldon on *The Big Bang Theory* seem manly.

Sarah had to admit she wanted that same happy glow

Charli wore on her face. She wanted to find her purpose, that special someone who would become the love of her life.

She wanted it all.

But so far, she hadn't done a darned thing to make it happen.

While she waited for Mrs. Chang to bring the bill for the Szechuan chicken that now lay like lead in her stomach alongside the bitter truth, she cracked open her fortune.

As the cookie crunched between her molars, she read the prophetic words that roared off that tiny scrap of paper.

If opportunity doesn't knock, build a door.

Her heart slammed against her ribs.

Message received.

Her life was a mess.

She was tired of being invisible. Tired of being alone. She was only twenty-eight years old. It was time for a change.

Ready to take action, she took a deep breath, threw a twenty-dollar bill down on the table, and busted that door wide open.

Chapter Two

TAKING A BIG leap worked out great if you were a flying squirrel. For a simple girl on a complex mission that took her way out of her comfort zone? That's where things got a little dicey.

Two months ago Sarah had decided if she was going to make a change it had to be supersized. Her leap had swung all the way into the state of Texas and the little ranching town of Sweet, where six months ago she'd arrived with the makeover show as Charli's personal assistant.

As the production crew had redesigned several buildings on Main Street and even the charming town square, Sarah had fallen in love with the place and the people.

If she'd been looking to spread her wings what better place to land?

Without a whole lot of thought so she didn't chicken out, she'd packed up her belongings, hooked up a small trailer to the back of her eight-year-old Ford Escape, and boldly interrupted her family's Sunday prayers to say ta-ta toodle-oo. Her announcement had barely garnered a blink.

Confirmation she'd made the right decision.

The drive from L.A. to Texas had been an adventure in independence she'd never forget. Along the way she learned how to change a tire, how to resist the temptation of gas-station-prepared hot dogs, and how many rest stops were between Phoenix and Tucson.

She'd also met up with an unexpected traveling companion in the form of an abandoned kitten at a travel center in Las Cruces. Because of the kitten's adorable white face and black ears that stood up like little wings, she'd had no choice but to adopt her and name her in honor of the place where she'd been rescued. With little Pilot as her co-pilot, the road trip became much less lonely.

Now, two months later, Sarah had a cozy place to live in Reno Wilder's barn apartment on Wilder Ranch. She'd also snapped up a job at Bud's Nothing Finer Diner, where the food was a treat for the taste buds, the pay fair, and the work comfortable for someone who'd slung hash all through college.

Bud's diner was the heartbeat of Sweet.

The patrons at Bud's made the work fun and helped Sarah feel like a part of the community. If there was gossip to be told, it happened at the big round table in the center of the diner. If a problem with city hall existed, the solutions were hashed out in a back booth. The *Don't Mess With Texas* signs and red-white-and-blue décor spoke volumes about the patriotic nature of the folks who sipped Bud's wicked java brew and dunked their fried pickles in a healthy splash of ranch dressing.

Bud's was nothing short of legendary.

And sometimes, on a sunny day like today, you might get to serve the hottest guy in town. Which, until now, was something Sarah had been too chicken to do.

"Sooo . . . Valentine's Day is a couple weeks away." Newlywed Paige Marshall flipped her long blond ponytail behind her back and reached for a menu and set of silverware. "What are your plans?"

Sarah balked. "Plans?"

Valentine's Day had always been the one holiday Sarah tried to ignore. The barrage of store decorations, flowers, and candy commercials made that all but impossible. Since her adolescent years, she'd spent the holiday alone. Well, except for the one year when, out of total desperation, she'd attended a "Stupid Cupid" party. The event had been an entertaining evening poking fun at the "celebration of love" with other singles who'd had the same "Valentine's Day sucks" viewpoint.

She'd still gone home alone.

This year, more than anything, she wanted the sugary pink-and-red holiday of love to be different.

"I know you're new in town," Paige said. "But is there someone special you'd like to celebrate with?"

Sarah adored Paige, who was a lot like Charli in the go-getter category. When her new husband, Aiden, had returned from the war after the loss of his best friends in battle, he'd been lost, guilt-ridden, and determined that he didn't deserve happiness. Paige changed his mind, and they were now one of the happiest couples Sarah had ever met.

"Someone special?"

Paige sighed. "Are you just going to repeat everything I say?"

"I'm sorry." She snapped her wandering mind back to the present. "I don't have any plans. And I really haven't been in town long enough to get to know anyone."

"Maybe this will change that." Paige pushed today's edition of the *Sweet Weekly Journal* across the counter. "Page two. Right hand column."

Curious, Sarah opened the paper.

Sweet's Valentine's Day Most Wanted

Expecting to see a list of floral suppliers and candy makers, Sarah was surprised to see a list of bachelors in the area along with the qualities they looked for in a woman.

She scanned the directory of names, which included the very handsome brothers Jesse and Jake Wilder, as well as Paige's brother-in-law Ben Marshall. But when her eyes landed on bachelor number four, she could swear she heard the ringing of a bell.

4. Deputy Brady Bennett

Ladies, check out Deputy Hot Stuff if you're looking for a man who knows his way around a pair of handcuffs.

Age: 33
Height: 6'2"
Hair: Light brown
Eyes: Leaf green
Qualities he looks for in a woman:
1. Confidence.
2. Adventurous.
3. Someone who will bring out the best in him.
4. Someone not afraid of a little friendly competition.
5. Cooking skills (since he says he can even burn a PB & J).

Sarah glanced up from the newspaper. Her gaze wandered out over the busy diner and landed on Deputy Brady Bennett, the hottest guy in town.

With or without a badge.

Tall, lean, and muscular, the man filled out a khaki uniform as tasty as a Snickers bar filled out a wrapper. Beneath the short sleeves, his biceps expanded without looking like he'd achieved them pumping iron in a gym. His broad shoulders and chest boosted the authority of the shiny star pinned to his pocket. His squared jaw, the intensity of his dark green eyes, and his warm brown hair screamed 100 percent virile male.

Sarah couldn't stop the little sigh that lifted from her chest.

A man that mouthwatering would never be interested in a woman like her.

Unless . . .

She glanced down at his wish list in the newspaper article.

Unless she . . .

1. Learned to rock the catwalk.
2. Jumped from an airplane or climbed Mt. Everest.
3. Convinced him he was already the best.
4. Put on a Texas Ranger's uniform and developed an RBI score.
5. Whipped up a batch of her killer spaghetti.

Number three would be no problem. All the man needed to do was look in the mirror. Number five could be accomplished by a simple trip to the grocery store. The rest were ridiculous.

She'd never been confident, adventurous, or an overly skilled athlete.

But she was willing to learn.

As discreetly as possible, she tore the article from the newspaper and tucked it into the pocket of her apron.

Maybe the question wasn't *what* she wanted to do on Valentine's Day but *who*.

Because really, when a girl decided to leap, it was go big or go home.

And going home was *not* an option.

As HE SAT down in the booth at Bud's Diner, Brady realized his life had become a pattern of rituals—breakfast at Bud's five times a week, dinner at Bud's four times a week, and near starvation on the remaining days.

Not that he couldn't cook; it was just that he had no idea what to cook other than scrambled eggs or tossing a tasteless frozen dinner in the microwave. Bud's served him a hot, delicious meal and he never had to eat alone. Although sometimes he preferred it.

Before a waitress could bring his set of silverware and the menu he could recite by heart, Ashley Jenkins, local realtor and the woman who'd *won* him with her high bid at the Black Ties and Levi's charity auction last year slid into the seat across from him.

Unfortunately, Ashley translated the word *won* to "own."

Not that she wasn't an attractive woman with her red hair and *Playboy* figure. Just that she was too overbearing and too overdone for his taste. He'd always preferred a woman who looked like she would be his best friend instead of a supermodel. The natural, girl-next-door type. Someone he could enjoy and laugh with who didn't worry that her makeup was smudged or the small dinner salad she'd ordered might make her fat.

Ashley did *not* fall into that category.

In her rush to launch herself into his booth and disrupt his solitary dining experience, she collided with the waitress bringing him his menu and silverware. As the utensils and glass crashed to the floor, water sloshed down the front of the waitress's uniform—a fitted white tee, black shorts, and red apron.

Unable to stop himself, his attention immediately went to the pink lace bra peeking through her wet T-shirt.

God, he was such a guy.

Lucky for him he was a guy with great eyesight.

The sudden commotion grabbed the interest of everyone within twenty feet. Which pretty much meant everyone in the diner.

He leveled a "move along folks, nothing to see here" nod just as Ashley growled and fired into a rant.

"Watch where you're going." Ashley brushed back the stiff curls that had dislodged from her heavily sprayed hairdo. "I mean really, it's not like you have such a difficult job that you can't see what's in front of you."

"I'm so sorry." With a look of humiliation and apology, the petite blonde waitress bent to pick up the mess.

Furious at Ashley's rude behavior, Brady slid from the booth and kneeled down to help.

"It wasn't your fault," he said, glancing into the piercing blue eyes she hid behind a pair of black-framed glasses.

"I should have been paying more attention." She shook her head, snatched up cubes of ice and broken shards, and plunked them into the jagged-edged glass. "I usually reserve my two left feet for dancing."

He chuckled and then took a good look at her face.

High cheekbones, luscious lips, and cute dimples. Totally the girl-next-door type.

Lucky him.

She ducked her head again, soaking up the water with a towel she'd had tucked in her apron.

"You've been avoiding me." He gave her a smile.

Her head came up, eyes wide. "I beg your pardon?"

"I come in here several times a week. This is the first you've even come close to my table. It's the badge, right? You're intimidated by cops. Maybe a con on the run?"

At his pathetic attempt at a joke, her gaze dropped to the star above his pocket, then shot back up to his face. "No. I'm . . . just . . ."

"Searching for something to say?"

The smile that lifted her lips nearly floored him.

"Beyond, 'Welcome to Bud's. My name is Sarah,' I'm probably not the world's best conversationalist," she admitted.

"Well, Sarah, maybe you just haven't found the right audience."

"Ummm. Hellooooo?" Ashley waved her red fingernails in front of his face. "Waiting here."

Brady looked up at his uninvited guest, carefully masking the irritation that pinched the back of his neck. In that split second, Sarah made a dash and disappeared into the kitchen.

With a long sigh, he returned to his seat and considered the woman across from him. Since her generous bid at the auction to support the expansion of the Sweet Emergency Center, Ashley had been trying to collect what she thought was her due.

Namely him.

In bed.

Not that he was against rolling in the sheets with a beautiful woman. He just didn't see her in that light. For his tastes she was too manipulative and self-serving.

He'd had enough of that kind of woman in his life.

No need to repeat his mistakes.

"I saw you on the 'Most Wanted' list in the newspaper," she said, giving him a little tsk-tsk. "I hope you'll remember that I get first dibs. After all, I did buy—"

The game had grown old.

He leaned over the table, and in a low voice told her, "You didn't *buy me*, Ashley. You donated to a local charity. In return, I took you to dinner, fixed the leak in your kitchen sink, and I escorted you to your sister's wedding, where you proceeded to get drunk and embarrass yourself. And me. I think we can safely say my debt has been paid."

She pursed her dark red lips. "I expected more."

"Sorry. I'm not for sale."

"Whatever." She slid out of the booth. "Maybe you should be a little more friendly like your buddies."

"They haven't slept with you either," a low voice growled.

Brady looked up at the man standing beside the booth. Jesse Wilder grinned down at the woman, who was definitely in a snit.

"And if I were you," Jesse added, "I wouldn't count on it happening anytime soon."

In a huff, Ashley stormed back to her own table and Brady sipped his now tepid coffee to hide a chuckle. Jesse plopped down into the seat across from him.

"Jesus, man." Jesse laughed. "It's barely sunup and you've already pissed off the female nation."

"Just sitting here minding my own business." Brady set down his cup. "And I hardly think *she* qualifies as the entire female nation."

"Might as well." Jesse chuckled. "By sundown, all of Sweet will know you're either questionably gay or suffering from erectile dysfunction."

"Would you like a cup of coffee, sir?"

Brady looked up to find Sarah standing beside their booth, steaming coffee carafe in hand. He hoped to God she hadn't heard Jesse's last four words.

"*Sir?*" Jesse grinned and turned on the infamous Wilder charm. "Darlin', it's just 'Jesse.' "

"I thought you preferred 'Dr. Wilder,' " Brady interjected, not liking the sudden interest in his friend's eyes.

"Only from those paying me for my services." He returned his attention to Sarah. "And yes. I would love a cup of coffee."

Brady watched her give Jesse an easy smile as she turned over his cup and filled it to the rim.

"Are you ready to order?" she asked, slipping a pad and pencil from her apron pocket.

Jesse ordered the Cattleman's Special—aka a heart attack on a plate. Brady went for broke and ordered cheesecake pancakes topped with fresh strawberries instead of sticking to the usual scrambled eggs and sourdough toast he made at home. Anything beyond that simple meal could mean a call to the volunteer fire department. Been there, done that. An episode in his life he wasn't proud of but had once needed to resort to. And had yet to live down.

"Anything else?" Sarah asked while she continued to scribble on the order pad like she was writing a journal entry.

He'd like her phone number, but then the image of how his last relationship had ended came crashing down and he simply shook his head.

He wasn't ready.

He might never be ready.

Still, he held his breath and waited for Jesse's response.

He might not be ready, but he wouldn't exactly choose to give his friend the green light to ask her out either.

Thankfully, Sweet's most infamous playboy simply pushed his cup toward the edge of the table and said, "More coffee when you get a chance."

She flashed them a smile as she turned on her pink sneakers and went to the kitchen to deliver their order.

Brady watched her go.

He watched the gentle sway of her hips beneath those short black shorts. Watched the muscles in her toned calves flex. Watched the white soles of her tennis shoes alternately flash against the black-and-white tile floor.

"Why her?"

Whipping his head back around, he found Jesse sitting there with a smirk. "What?"

"Why. *Her*?"

Fighting the temptation to turn and look again, Brady kept his eyes forward. "Don't know what you're talking about."

"Yeah." Jesse leaned back and stretched his arm along the top of the seat. "Heard that one before." He glanced over his shoulder. "It's good to have you back."

"You always talk in code?" Brady sipped his quickly cooling coffee. "Back where?"

"Among the living. Thought for sure Andrea had killed you for good."

If the time of year wasn't bad enough, just the sound of her name made Brady cringe.

It didn't matter that the newspaper had seen fit to add him to their "Most Wanted" bachelor list; he had no intention of setting himself up to be betrayed again.

And in no uncertain terms would he ever again do Valentine's Day.

Chapter Three

SARAH DIDN'T UNDERSTAND why she'd suddenly developed springs on her feet. They didn't make the huge leaps she kept taking any easier.

Or less foolish.

Sunrise had not yet peaked over the hilltops as she sat in her Ford Escape on a quaint tree-lined street in the middle of a neighborhood that boasted a pond, playground, and walking paths. Soon the families who lived on this street would awaken and start the day with kisses and hugs while she sat outside Brady Bennett's house like some kind of pathetic stalker.

Sure, she knew the polite term was *secret admirer*, but when a person found themselves sneaking down a dark street so they could anonymously place a gift inside a mailbox, *stalker* seemed more appropriate.

The idea had formulated over the past twenty-four

hours since she'd finally come face-to-face with him in the diner. She'd been tongue-tied and embarrassed when he'd kneeled down to help her pick up the broken glass. She'd also looked into his intense dark green eyes and found herself imagining all kinds of crazy things.

Deputy Bennett inspired hot, sweaty thoughts.

He was also a man who inspired thoughts of heart and home, although Sarah knew better than to allow herself such frivolous notions. Chances were a man like him would never waste a passing moment on a woman like her, but that didn't mean she wouldn't give it a go.

Not that she was a one-night-stand kind of girl, but even having the opportunity to say no was more appealing than sitting home alone night after night with nothing but the TV and her kitten for company.

To say she had professional skills in the kitchen was an overstatement. But she was determined and, yeah, okay, maybe a little desperate. So when the idea to tease Deputy Bennett with a few secret messages entered her mind, she grabbed hold with both hands.

And then she promptly shoved them into a bowl of batter.

If the way to a man's heart was through his stomach, she intended to entice the core of that handsome man with a little sugar and a lot of mystery.

AS ONE OF the single guys on the force, Brady often pulled swing or graveyard shift. Both could be on the boring side as the sidewalk in Sweet usually rolled up around dark, leaving only the deer, armadillos, and a few rebellious teens to wreak havoc. Unlike his friends who sought out new adventures or were tying the knot, his work routine—like his life—had become a lackluster case of the same old-same old. Maybe he needed to figure out a way to spice it up.

On yet another sunny day, he strolled to the mailbox to grab yet another handful of bills before heading out to keep peace among the peaceful.

"Hey, handsome."

Brady looked up to catch the wink tossed by Megan Walsh as she rode by at max speed on her cyclo-cross bike. Megan—a competitive cyclist—had buns and abs of steel that put his own to shame. And he was pretty fit. She also had an eye out for a submissive man whose biggest ambition was to hang out in the spectator stands and cheer her on. He'd found out the hard way that Megan had a dominatrix alter ego. And since he was the kind of guy who believed handcuffs only belonged on criminals, He and Megan just didn't fit.

Thank God.

He gave her a courtesy wave then reached inside his mailbox. When he pulled out the stack of envelopes, a huge chocolate dipped fortune cookie wrapped in heart-dotted cellophane sat on top. A generous splash of classic Valentine-colored sprinkles decorated the thick layer of chocolate. He checked the bundle of mail for a note from the sender but found none. Obviously it been hand delivered.

It looked delicious. But could he really bring himself to eat something left in his mailbox by God-knew who? It could be laced with strychnine or XTC—a known sexual enhancer for those who dabbled in the S & M world.

Looking up, he caught Megan's pedaling backside. He waited for her to turn around and smile, indicating the surprise was from her, but she kept going until she turned the corner and was out of sight.

Hmmm.

He held up the cellophane-wrapped gift and looked at the cookie again. No doubt he was probably overthinking the whole thing. Not uncommon for someone who had to be so detail oriented on the job.

Still, could he really eat it?

On the way back to his front door he tore open the wrapper, cracked the cookie open, and pulled out the little rectangle of paper.

A pleasant surprise is in store for you.

There were few things Brady detested. The only one that came to mind was surprises. Especially surprises like the one his ex-fiancée had sprung on him last Valentine's Day.

He crumpled the cookie and the fortune in his hand.

No surprises.

No Valentine's Day.

No more catching him off guard.

The next time someone snuck a *surprise* in his mailbox, he'd be ready for them.

WHEN TO-DO LISTS became too long, you had to put things in gear just to check them off. On the way to work, Brady had already stopped by the Lost Sock to drop off his uniforms to be laundered, the Fuel Stop to refresh his protein powder supply, and Parks and Rec to sign up for the men's competitive spring softball league. Last on his list was Marshall's Sporting Goods to look for a new glove to replace the one he'd shredded last season.

He parked his Silverado in the small lot and checked out the new window display of athletic shoes, balance trainers, and yoga mats. The bell over the glass door chimed his appearance and his friend Ben Marshall popped out from the back room.

"Hey Deputy Dog, what's up?"

"Just signed up for spring ball," Brady said, scanning the long glass display case that held some high-end fishing reels. "Looking for a new glove."

"The long satin kind? Or would you prefer lacy fingerless style so they don't interfere with handcuffing a perp?"

"Always gotta be a smartass." Brady laughed despite his irritation. Ben and his brother Aiden had been his friends since they'd raced tricycles. Aiden, like several of his other friends, had recently gotten married. Which left Ben trying to figure out who should land on his "must harass" list for the day.

"I've got some new Wilson A2k series in the back room. Just opened the crate this morning," Ben said. "Give me a minute while I finish up with the knock-out blonde I'm helping."

"If it only takes you a minute, you're getting old, my friend."

"Ha." Ben pointed at him. "You're just wishing you were in my shoes."

Brady glanced toward the shoe room. "Who is it you're hiding back there?"

"She's new. And don't get any ideas. She's mine."

New?

An onslaught of tingles double-dipped his stomach.

If Ben was talking about a certain blonde waitress, Brady was throwing up a roadblock.

"The hell she is." Brady pushed past him and headed toward the back room where he found Sarah bent over tying a pair of pink-and-black softball cleats. Her long ponytail was hanging upside down and he couldn't help but notice how good she looked from behind in that position.

"You play ball?" he asked.

Startled, she looked up. Then a soft smile tilted those luscious lips. "Slow pitch, soccer, and volleyball."

No wonder she was so fit.

"If you tell me you watch football and hockey I might have to kiss you."

Her blue eyes brightened behind those black-framed glasses. "Denver Broncos and the Boston Bruins."

"Seriously?"

She righted herself and wiggled her toes beneath the shoe leather. "Is it written somewhere that only boys can like sports?"

He took a step back, floored by the fact that she could be beautiful *and* willing to crack the bat too. "No. I just don't meet very many women who do."

"Then you've been meeting the wrong women."

No shit.

Ben burst into the room. "Dammit, Bennett. Am I too late?"

"You're just in time," Sarah said. "These fit perfectly. I'll take them."

Impressed, Brady folded his arms and rocked back on his heels. "So you signed up for the slow pitch league?"

She nodded. "After I got off work."

"And you work where?" Ben asked, kneeling down to help her remove the cleats.

"Bud's Diner," she said, slipping her feet back into her pink sneakers.

"How did I not know that?" Ben asked.

"Because, as always," Brady said, "you're one step behind the rest of us."

"Damn. I hate when that happens." Ben stuck Sarah's new cleats back in the box and stood. "I'll have these up front at the counter when you're ready." He gave Brady a friendly shot to the shoulder on his way out the door.

"So what else are you good at?" he asked as she gathered up her purse.

"I never said I was any good." Her laugh was low and sexy for someone who looked like the girl next door. "But I have been known to haunt a billiards room or two before."

"So you're a shark?" He couldn't stop the grin that spread across his face.

"More like a guppy." As she moved past him on her way to the front of the store she smelled like lemony sunshine. A wonderfully fresh scent, and a relief from the heavy perfumes some women chose to wear.

"Then how about a match?" He followed her through the door. "Ten bucks to the winner."

She narrowed those big baby blues even as a smile lifted her lips. "So who's really the shark?"

"I pretty much suck." Lifting his hands, he laughed. "Ben can verify that as he's the last one who took my money after a lousy bank shot."

At the counter, she opened her purse, pulled out her wallet, and handed Ben her credit card.

"It's true." Ben took the card and held her gaze a bit longer than was customary. When Brady looked down, Ben was holding her hand too. "He sucks."

A wave of jealousy Brady had no right to feel crashed over him. "Maybe you have a few tricks up your sleeve you can show me?" he said to her.

"What do you mean?" Her tone grew edgy.

"Nothing major." He shrugged. "Maybe a cut shot or a foot shot."

Her delicate brows pulled together. "I don't even know what those are."

"Then maybe I can teach you."

"Dude." Ben handed back her credit card. "No hitting on the customers."

Busted. Brady chuckled to hide the obvious. "Just looking for a better pool partner than you."

"Uh-huh."

"So what do you say?" While Ben slipped her cleats into a bag, Brady took advantage. "I'm off tomorrow. How about a game at Seven Devils around eight?"

While she hesitated, she snagged her full bottom lip between her teeth. That simple action tugged something very complex in his lower body.

"Come on." He smiled. "I'm harmless."

"No, he's not," Ben interjected.

Her wary blue gaze slid from Ben back to him.

"I'll even spot you the ten bucks," he said, trying to tempt her into saying yes.

"I'm not worried about the money." She gave him a look he couldn't read. Then she picked up her purchase and headed toward the door, which she opened. She turned with a smile. "Because I don't intend to lose."

COMPOSURE WAS ALL a state of mind.

Sarah managed to keep it together as she walked out of the sporting-goods store, knowing both the store owner and Deputy Hot Stuff were watching.

She managed to appear cool, calm, and collected as she got up into her SUV, backed out of the parking space, and drove away.

It wasn't until she turned the corner of Main and River Streets that she pulled over, put the vehicle in park, and then proceeded to bend over with her head between her knees so she didn't pass out.

Good God, what had she gotten herself into?

She didn't flirt. But she'd just made an attempt that probably had left Brady laughing.

She didn't set up billiards dates with hot law-enforcement guys. And she'd be delusional to even imagine that he saw it as a date anyway.

Above all, she didn't pretend that she was anything other than just plain Sarah.

Yeah. And how had that been working for her?

Number three on Brady Bennett's qualities he looked for in a woman said he wanted someone who would bring out the best in him.

Maybe she needed someone to bring out the best in *her*.

Maybe he'd even be willing to teach her how to achieve the perfect kiss shot.

In the meantime, while she needed some serious girl advice, the last females on earth she'd ever ask would be her pious sisters. No, this time she needed a few words of wisdom from women who'd broken the rules, turned on their charm, and snagged the man of their dreams.

Sarah had lived in the fantasy realm long enough. She wanted someone she could wrap her arms around. Someone to hold on to, take care of, and find love with.

A little skin-to-skin action wouldn't be so bad either.

Chapter Four

WEEKNIGHTS AT SEVEN DEVILS Saloon were relatively mild compared to the weekends. The bar stools were usually taken by those with odd days off like him, or they were just hard-hitting drinkers.

Brady stood in the back room, holding the table he'd snagged as soon as he'd walked into the place. He'd already had to turn down game offers. One from Priscilla Barnes, who'd had a few too many brewskis and had been barely able to stand up. Another from Lila Ridenbaugh, who by all rights should have been home with her ever-growing brood of kids. Brady made a mental note to do a knock-and-talk on her door just to make sure those kids were being well taken care of. Not that he had any interest in becoming baby daddy number ten or twelve or whatever number Lila was currently trying to snag.

Still, even as he prepared to take a little break from

reality, he couldn't get his mind off the gift-wrapped fortune cookie he'd discovered on his front step when he'd gone home last night after work. It had been just after midnight. Exhaustion had taken its toll and he'd almost kicked the cellophane bag bearing pink hearts across his porch. Though unease had curled up his spine, he hadn't been able to resist seeing what message was wrapped up inside. He'd torn open the package, cracked the cookie in half, and pulled out the fortune.

Do something unusual in the coming days.

Unusual?

Yeah. The cookies had to be from Megan Walsh. She must be looking for a new BDSM plaything. Too bad she was barking up the wrong pair of handcuffs. He didn't do *unusual* if it came in the form of whips, chains, and slave collars.

No thanks.

He was just a regular guy.

According to his former fiancée, he was romantic—whatever the hell that meant. Too bad that in their relationship dollar signs superseded passion.

He'd have to have a little chat with Megan and tell her he had no intention of donning anything leather other than the jacket he wore when he rode his Harley.

Tearing his thoughts from the absurd, he brought his mind back to a much sweeter thought. Rummaging through the house pool sticks, he chose the two straightest to make sure his friendly competition with Sarah was as even as possible.

Not that he intended to play fair.

A gentleman always let the lady win.

He thought back to seeing her the day before and wasn't surprised when something fluttered through his stomach. That had been happening ever since she'd finally come to his table at Bud's. Something about her had definitely tickled his curiosity even as he knew he should ignore the attraction. With his history he didn't do permanent.

Sarah wasn't a temporary kind of girl.

She seemed sweet and untainted. Both were definite reasons he should back away. Yet something about her pushed him forward. Something he couldn't resist.

Billy Currington's "Hey Girl" played over the sound system while he chalked the cues.

Something tingled at the back of his neck. He looked up just as she appeared beneath the yellow-and-red glow of a neon sign.

Till now he'd seen her with her hair pulled back in a ponytail, wearing her Bud's Diner uniform of black shorts, white , and pink sneakers. Her bright blue eyes were always hidden behind a pair of black eyeglass frames.

The Sarah who came through the rough-hewn posts wearing a torn pair of painted-on jeans, a "MAMA TRIED" white tank, and a pair of cowboy boots made his jaw drop. Her long blond hair fell in big loose waves over her slim shoulders in a style that looked a little wild and crazy, and there were no glasses to cover up those vivid blue eyes.

Damn.

Had he seriously thought she was the girl next door?

Well, maybe she was, but with a whole lot of sexy added on top. Like the sweet, juicy cherry on top of a sundae.

"Hey." Okay, probably not the most intellectual greeting he'd ever spoken, but she definitely had him a little tongue-tied. "What's that?" He moved closer, inhaled her sweet lemony scent, and pointed to the leather case in her hand.

"It's my Outlaw."

"You have your own pool cue?"

She grinned. "You don't?"

"Shark." Returning her grin, he pointed at her. "I knew it."

What he hadn't known that first morning they'd met was how much fun she'd turn out to be.

"All right then." He grabbed one of the crappy sticks he'd culled from the bunch. "Let's play this one out. See where it goes."

Despite the warnings in his head, he hoped it would go far.

SHAKING IN THE boots she'd bought at Abby Morgan's rescue center thrift shop Sarah tried to remain composed as she removed her pool cue from the case. Amid the crack of balls from the other tables, the music, and the constant hum of chatter, she smoothed her palm over the branded wood and the smooth leather wrap, seeking some kind of tranquility in the familiarity.

Learning to play pool had been the only way she could get her three older brothers to pay her any attention. Unfortunately she'd been a good student, and when she began to trounce them, they pretended she didn't exist. Nothing new in her family. Still, it stung because she'd idolized them for as long as she could remember. Since then she'd learned to always let the male ego claim victory. Even if she could conquer him with the cue tied behind her back.

If she even survived this night without making a complete fool of herself it would be a miracle. She'd needed help, and she hadn't hesitated to ask for it. This morning she'd run into Charli on her way out of the apartment, which took up the entire upper level of Reno and Charli's barn. She told her former boss of the tight spot she'd gotten herself into. Charli had made a call to Paige, and between the two women, Sarah had been schooled all day in the art of getting your flirt on—Texas style.

In the words of her friends, Texas women were big-haired, stronger-than-an-armadillo's-back, take-no-prisoners kinds of females with soft hearts who had a knack for making sweet tea that would make your taste buds sing.

Sarah wanted to do them proud.

Most of all, she wanted to grab Brady's attention so he'd find her interesting and not the dull little mouse she'd been for way too long.

She looked up to find him watching her, green eyes dark and intense. Immediately her nerves bulldozed everything she'd been taught earlier in the day.

"Is something wrong?" she asked.

"That's an interesting way to handle that thing."

She glanced at the long shaft, rubbed her hand over the wooden surface. "It's like an old friend."

"I am so screwed. And maybe a little turned on." He slapped a ten-dollar bill on the corner of the table. "How about you rack and break, Little Miss I-Don't-Know-How-to-Play?"

"I never said I didn't know how to play." She laid her ten on top of his, chalked her cue, and pulled up her big-girl pants. "I just didn't know the terms you used. No one ever taught me the terminology."

"You insinuated."

"I think telling you I had no intention of losing was anything but insinuation that I didn't know how to play." She blew the excess chalk away. "You want to back out?"

"Hell no."

"Good." Blinking against the glare of the red Budweiser hanging billiard light, she leaned over the table and settled the rack into place. She could feel the heat of his gaze slide up and down her behind. Not that she minded. She'd never had a man look at her the way Brady did. Then again, that could just be a figment of her overzealous imagination.

Nerves danced through her stomach and she conjured up the magical words of encouragement she'd earlier been given. With a total lack of finesse she dove headfirst into the flirting pool.

"Are you staring at my backside?"

"Oh yeah." His response was a low and sexy affirmation that whipped her dancing nerves into a frenzy.

A smile crossed her lips as she silently thanked her mentors for steering her in the right direction on what to wear and how to strap on the sass. She was actually flirting, and it was turning out to be fun. Of course she needed a whole lot of practice and as Charli said, backslides were entirely possible.

"Just remember," she said, "turnabout is fair play."

"Duly noted." He cleared his throat. "So . . . you want something to drink?"

"Other than a glass of wine now and again I've never been much of a drinker." She righted herself and caught him eyeing her in a way that sent a barrage of tingles through her midsection.

"Soda then?" His head cocked just enough to make it feel like a dare.

"I'll have what you're having."

That deep green gaze lowered to the longneck bottle in his big hand then climbed up the front of her shirt until they locked eyes. "It's pretty smooth. You might like it."

She did like it. She'd be a fool not to.

While he flagged the waitress, she leaned down and busted the rack apart with a wide break shot that sank the two ball in the corner pocket.

"Yep." He gave a slow shake of his head. "Screwed."

"I promise not to take advantage."

At least not without his permission.

"Sarah?"

She looked up and found the guy she'd met at the Wilder party, when the TV show had been filming, walking toward her. With stacked Wranglers over his boots and a straw hat low over his forehead, he was still as handsome as the moment she'd met him. He'd shown her some attention, but over the days of filming she'd quickly realized that he was quite popular with the ladies. And in her book, why stand in line to get your heart broken?

While she might be in the process of taking huge leaps of faith, she didn't want to be just another notch on someone's bedpost.

"Zack! How are you?"

Ignoring Brady, Zack walked up and hugged her like they were old friends. "What are you doing here?"

She glanced at Brady who, oddly, did not appear happy. Maybe Zack was a known troublemaker Brady had dealt with while on the job. Otherwise, why such a scowl?

"I moved here a couple of months ago."

"Why?" Zack tilted the straw hat back on his head. "Couldn't see the stars in L.A.?"

"Production closed down. Recession put a squelch on high-cost reality shows." She shrugged. "I guess I was just looking for a new adventure."

"I'd be happy to offer my services." His grin suggested there was more than just a welcome wagon behind his words.

"I think she's tied up at the moment," Brady finally said in a tone that implied Zack might want to take his offer elsewhere.

Zack slid a look in Brady's direction that definitely indicated there was some bad blood between the two. "Just trying to be friendly, Deputy."

Sarah glanced from one man to the other and swore the heavy weight of testosterone tipped the scales. Whatever it was between these two, she didn't want to be in the middle.

"I appreciate the thought, Zack." She pasted on a pleasant smile. "Maybe we can talk another time. Deputy Bennett and I were just—"

"Yeah. I got that." Zack tipped his hat. "Another time then."

As he walked away, Sarah released a breath. Then she looked back to Brady, who watched Zack walk away. She was afraid to ask why the dark look but curiosity got the best of her.

"I take it you don't care for him," she said.

"Does it show?"

"Like a bad sunburn."

Ignoring her initial comment, Brady sipped his bottle of Shiner Bock then turned his frown right side up. "You ready to play?"

She nodded.

"Well, let's go then."

Even with three brothers she knew she'd never understand the nature of men and their complexities. For now, she was just happy to be standing in the presence of one so gorgeous and thanking her lucky stars she wasn't home watching *How I Met Your Mother* reruns.

She leaned in, formed a bridge with her hand, pulled back the stick, and thrust. Before the tip even met the hard ball she knew the shot would be off and would miss the pocket by a mere inch.

"Darn."

His brows pulled together. "You did that on purpose."

"I said I could play. Not that I played perfectly."

He came close enough that she caught the scent of warm skin and clean cotton.

"You play to win." He tucked his knuckles beneath her chin and gently lifted so she had no choice but to look up and catch the flecks of gold sparking in his eyes.

For a moment she thought, wondered, hoped that he might kiss her. But she supposed that would be expecting too much. She didn't even know him, and vice versa. And while he had "good time guaranteed" written all over that mouthwatering body, he appeared to be a bit cautious even as he opened the door to his Southern hospitality. Since she was a logical girl, she figured that's all that was going on here. Hospitality.

"Got that?" he added.

She loaded a barrel with an offer he couldn't refuse, and pointed it directly at the alpha male in him just dying to get out.

"You want a fair game?" she said, knowing a true alpha never backed down from a challenge. "Then how about we up the ante?"

One side of his mouth curled in a wry smile. "You talking money?"

She lifted a shoulder. "Your call."

Thick biceps bulged beneath the soft gray plaid flannel as his arms folded across a muscular chest her fingers itched to reach out and touch.

"You ever rode a motorcycle?" he asked.

Uh-oh.

"Never."

"Then you lose? You learn."

"Meaning?"

"Tomorrow you go for a ride with me and I will teach you."

While the idea of having her arms wrapped around that hot muscular body did crazy things to her lady parts, the idea of trying to hold up the huge motorcycle she'd seen him cruise by the diner on petrified her.

She gasped. "You want me to ride the big one?"

The grin that broke across his face indicated she might not have chosen her words carefully.

"How about we start out slow," he said. "Take it easy. Then once you get the feel of it, we go for broke."

"Ummmm."

"Come on, trash talker." He leaned close and chuckled. "You in or not?"

"In." She pointed to the table. "Now put your money where your mouth is. You're stripes."

Grin still in place, he pushed up the long sleeves of the flannel shirt that hung unbuttoned over a V-neck T-shirt. The white cotton fit snug, but the tails of the flannel hung loose around his lean hips. When he leaned over the table and lined up the shot she developed a new appreciation for well-worn Levis.

He formed a bridge and slid the stick between his thumb and finger. When he pulled back his arm and delivered the shot, the ten and the fourteen balls dropped neatly into a side and a corner pocket.

Scarlet and amber illumination from the hanging light cast a glow on the right side of his face as he turned and flashed a smile that ignited the intensity in his green eyes.

Desire twisted her stomach into a knot and her heart took a crazy sidestep.

She was in way over her head.

And it had nothing at all to do with playing pool.

Chapter Five

NORMALLY TWO DAYS off were too many. Brady often found himself bored or lonely and looking for company. He was thankful for his close circle of friends, but two of them had just gotten engaged and now spent more time with their women than with the guys. Not that he blamed them. It just narrowed his options.

This morning, however, as he rolled out of bed, he had something to look forward to.

Last night's pool competition had been fun and more than just the break from boredom he'd expected. Sarah wasn't a natural flirt. In fact, one might say she was a bit on the clumsy side. But she'd put her heart into it and he'd been charmed. Right up until the moment Zack Gifford had invaded his space.

Brady had never been the type to hold a grudge . . . until his former fiancée decided to turn his world on its head. Zack had unwittingly inserted himself into her fall from grace. And though she'd played the younger man like a professional, Brady just couldn't find it in his cold heart to feel sorry.

Today, things were looking up.

He didn't need to be a one-man welcoming committee and show Sarah the highlights of living in Sweet, but he'd never considered himself a dope. Thus he planned to take full advantage of getting to know sweet Sarah before all the horndogs, like Ben, in town caught her scent.

She'd lost the game last night. He wasn't sure she used all her billiards skills, but he'd take the win if it meant he got to spend a little more one-on-one with her.

He rinsed his plate of scrambled-egg scraps—the one thing he managed to cook without charring it beyond recognition—and set it in the dishwasher. With a few hours to kill before he picked up Sarah, he went out to grab the newspaper to make sure nothing had rattled the little town of Sweet while he'd been sleeping.

As soon as he opened the door he spotted the heart-dotted cellophane-wrapped fortune cookie on the doormat. He jerked his gaze to the street to see if he could catch Megan or whoever had left it on his front step. But the only breathing soul around was Mrs. Cronerbee's orange tabby cat Meowser, who gave Brady a look, flicked his tail, then tore his claws into the oak tree in Brady's front yard. Within seconds he was glaring down at Brady from the first branch. Brady usually tried to give the cat a scratch beneath the chin but it appeared Meowser was in fine form today and preferred to play.

Brady reached down and picked up the cookie. He definitely needed to have a talk with Megan. No sense letting her think anything between them was possible.

The same as the others, the cookie appeared to be homemade, not store-bought. And just as before, he gave it about two seconds' consideration before he tore open the cellophane, cracked open the giant-sized cookie, and pulled out the fortune.

A small incident will develop to your advantage.

He popped a piece of cookie into his mouth as he grabbed the paper off the porch and headed back into the house. In his experience there were no *small* incidents. Most all led to something bigger and often became a big disadvantage.

And he wanted no part of that action.

As SHE WAITED for Brady to arrive, Sarah pulled Pilot onto her lap and stroked the silky soft fur between the kitten's little black ears.

Anticipation and anxiety clashed in her stomach and she wondered about the expression *nervous as a cat*. Pilot, who was purring her little heart out, seemed quite calm. She, on the other hand, felt like she was coming apart at the seams.

"Why are you so nervous?" Charli paused from the cosmetic makeover she insisted would give Sarah a boost of confidence. "Apparently you made a great impression last night, because he asked you out for a second date."

"It's not a date," Sarah insisted. "I lost the game."

The corners of Charli's mouth lifted. "Did you?"

"Yes." She rubbed her nose to dislodge the fluff of kitten fur that had floated up.

"In any case," Charli said as she teased the living daylights out of Sarah's hair, "he put out the idea, which means he's interested. So why are you so nervous?"

The fact that she'd never been anywhere near a motorcycle of any kind in her entire life wasn't necessarily the biggest issue. Being with Brady one-on-one without benefit of distraction from diner customers, sporting-goods shop owners, or saloon partiers rated at the top of OMG! Right alongside the outfit Charli had picked out for her to wear.

Sarah had to quit looking in the mirror.

The Daisy Dukes—which hardly seemed proper attire for motorcycle riding—were on loan from her former boss, who swore the inky-dinky denims and silver Texas belt buckle had secret powers. The tank top came from her own closet, and the boots were a rerun of the night before.

"I look like a floozy."

"Who uses that word?" Charli snorted a laugh. "Don't you ever watch CMT? Haven't you seen any Luke Bryan or Jason Aldean videos? Southern boys love this look."

"It's stereotypical," Sarah insisted.

"It will get you laid. I guarantee it."

Sarah gasped so hard she choked and Pilot skittered off her lap. "I'm not out to get laid."

"Honey, we're all out to get laid." Charli patted her shoulder. "Let me rephrase that with we're all out to get laid by the right guy. No one's accusing you of being . . ."

"A floozy?"

Charli laughed. "Yes. That. You're looking for more than just hopping into bed with a guy. But it never hurts to put a little spit on the shine."

"Eeew."

"You know what I mean." Charli set the teasing comb down on the bathroom counter and turned Sarah toward the mirror. "You look awesome."

"Ummm." She'd never had hair so big.

"You know the higher the hair the closer to God."

"But I'll most likely be wearing a helmet."

"Yeah. *After* you knock his socks off."

"I'm just—"

"Trust me. Desperate times call for desperate measures."

"I never said I was desperate."

"We all are at one time or other. Don't feel bad if the description fits. Now stand up and let me take a final look."

Charli made a little turnaround motion with her hand. Sarah reluctantly complied.

"Perfect." Charli gave a sharp nod of her head. "Brady Bennett is not going to know what hit him. Now let me get out of here before he arrives. Remember to flirt your ass off. Be confident. And . . . what was number two on his list?" She tapped her chin. "Oh yeah, be adventurous."

With a quick kiss to Sarah's cheek, Charli was out the door and Sarah was left in "what the hell did I get myself into?" mode.

All in all the outrageous outfit did nothing to deter her from the anticipation of seeing Brady again. And though she wasn't ready to reveal herself as his secret admirer, she hoped he was enjoying the carefully thought out fortunes she'd been inserting into his cookies.

SOME DAYS WERE perfect for picnics, or watching movies, or sitting on the front porch as the world passed by. Brady smiled as he parked his truck next to Reno Wilder's barn. The day was warm with a cloudless blue sky. Perfect for kicking up a little dust. Not that he would particularly mind watching movies in the dark with a beautiful woman at his side.

The beautiful woman who'd been on his mind for the past few days came out from the dark of the barn and, once again, made his jaw drop.

Had he really thought she was the girl-next-door type?

He pulled the keys from the ignition and watched her walk toward his truck.

Yeah, she still was, but with an extra something that promised life with her would never be dull. She continued to peak his interest. Hell, according to the dream he'd had of her last night he didn't stand a chance in hell if she decided she wanted him as more than just a good old Southern boy tour guide.

He wanted to know more about her than just that she looked sexy as hell in those cut-off jeans. He wanted to know where she came from other than just Los Angeles. What made her tick? What were her deepest hopes, dreams, and desires? And how might he be able to help her fulfill them?

Yeah. He was in deep trouble.

He slid out of the truck. "You look great."

She glanced down at herself. When her face tilted back up toward the sun, a telling flush rushed to her cheeks.

The outfit hadn't been her idea.

He glanced across the gravel driveway at the comfortable home his friend Reno and the woman who'd managed to heal his heart now shared. The ensemble had Charli's bold and lively style written all over it. Brady would have to thank her later. For now he just intended to enjoy the day.

And the company.

"I don't think these shorts are going to work very well for *those*." She pointed to the two Kawasaki bikes in his truck bed.

Maybe not. But they were working great for him.

"Tell you what. How about you just run inside and grab a pair of jeans and a hoodie and bring them along just in case."

"Will there be somewhere I can change?"

Honey, you don't need to change. Just keep that sweet thing going. It's working.

"I promise to close my eyes."

"Oh."

Obviously a little dazed, she turned and headed back into the barn and the apartment on the top floor. Instinct sent him after her.

She'd left the door open and he walked inside, taking

note of the changes in the apartment since Jackson Wilder had moved out. Namely, the place smelled like a woman. Fresh powder, scented candles, and maybe a hint of warm vanilla body lotion.

As a law enforcement officer he'd trained himself to use his sensory perception on crime scenes. Mostly he used his acute sense of smell to scope out DUI's who thought they could mask the stench of whiskey with spearmint gum.

The other changes to the apartment were in the sense of homey touches added to the leather furniture in the form of a quilt over the back of the sofa and pillows with bold prints. Fresh flowers sat in the center of the dining-room table, breakfast bar, and coffee table. He thought of his own home and the obvious man-cave appearance. It wasn't that he hadn't had time to decorate, or that his mom and sister hadn't offered to lend a hand, it was that he'd hoped his fiancée—before she'd become his ex—would have put her touches on it. He'd hoped they could have built that house into a home.

Since she'd taken her *talents* elsewhere, he had no desire to cozy-up the place. The cold interior was a reminder of the days following her betrayal when he wasn't sure he could hold his head up and carry on. Somehow he'd survived, all thanks, he knew, to his family and friends, who never gave up on him.

Something tickled his ankles. He looked down. The tiniest black-and-white kitten looked up at him with big blue eyes and gave him a squeaky meow. "Hey, little guy." He reached down and picked up the bundle of fur.

"That's Pilot." Sarah came back into the room with a

small bag stuffed with what he imagined held her necessary change of clothes. "I found her beside a Dumpster at a travel center in Las Cruces."

"She's pretty small to be left all alone like that," he said, stroking the kitten, who easily fit into one of his hands.

"That's what I thought." Sarah stepped closer. "There's no way I could have left her there to fend for herself." She reached out and stroked the kitten from head to tail. Their hands met on top of all that soft fur and a quiver ran down his back.

Pretty sure it wasn't from the cat.

He tried not to let Sarah's warm, generous heart wrap around him like a blanket. Tried not to inhale deeper just to catch her sweet scent. Tried not to let his heart engage with his curiosity. Tried not to let his body react.

Yeah.

He tried.

When she looked up at him and smiled he knew he'd have to try harder. Because at the moment, he was ten kinds of gone.

"You got everything?" he asked, amazed he could keep his voice from cracking.

"I think so."

He put the kitten down, gave it another little stroke over the top of its head, then fought reaching down to take Sarah's hand.

What he'd thought would be just a fun little adventure was going to be a lesson in restraint.

AMIDST A VAST landscape dotted with rolling hills, scrub, and cacti, Sarah studied the dirt bike with great consternation. While trying out new things might be the reason she'd moved to Texas, the contraption she was supposed to climb on looked like a motorized death sentence. Or at the very least a broken arm or leg waiting to happen.

"Nervous?" Brady stood beside her with one hand on the bike grip, explaining to her about kick starts, and shifters, and easing off the clutch so you didn't pop it and end up on the ground. His other hand was settled at the small of her back.

The first gave her jitters.

The second gave her shivers.

"Kind of."

One corner of his sensuous mouth lifted. "I promise we'll take this slow and easy. You can count on me."

She allowed her gaze to roam over his big, strong body. Even without the uniform and badge, he did indeed look like someone she could depend on. Whether it was from the sincerity shining in his dark eyes, or just the encouragement in his deep voice, she couldn't tell. Her heart, which happened to be doing a whole lot of skipping around, didn't seem to care.

"I trust you." She swallowed down her fear and her increasing attraction to this man. "Should I get on now?"

"You might want to change into your long jeans first."

"I'm just trying to learn how to use the controls for now. I'll change when I get that figured out."

"You sure?"

She nodded. Took a deep breath and climbed on. Warmed by the sun, the seat stung her bare legs. Maybe she should have taken his advice. The last thing she wanted to do was sound like a whiny baby, so she ignored the sting and looked up at him for further instructions.

After he'd explained the whole easing off the clutch thing a couple of times, she still couldn't grasp the concept. Much to her delight, he climbed on and sat behind her. Built for one, the seat forced them to sit close. Really close. Like her bottom pressed against his generous package close.

Not that she minded.

He leaned in and pressed his chest to her back while his arms surrounded her and his hands covered hers on top of the handle grips. Comfortably caged between him and the bike she had a hard time focusing on his instructions to push here, let off there, and step on this. The whole time his words rumbled deep in his chest and vibrated against her back. She could listen to him talk all day. But what she really wanted to do was turn around, wrap her arms and legs around him, and see where they went from there.

Though she had little experience with men, she'd had enough to know that no man had ever turned her on the way he did. And before she got her hopes up or allowed her anticipation to peak any higher, she put a cap on all the wild, crazy, and very hot images going through her mind.

"Think you've got it now?" he asked.

Saying yes would mean he'd move away. "Maybe you could go over that just one more time?"

"Sure. It's all about safety."

He leaned in again and she managed not to purr. But she did draw the line at trying to pretend it was all about safety. At the moment it was all about lust.

Distracted, she didn't listen much better this time, but really, how hard could it be? "I think I've got it," she said.

"You sure?"

She nodded and as he got off the bike, she instantly was sorry she hadn't played dumb at least one more time. He walked to the truck and came back with a helmet that he set over her head. As he pulled the strap beneath her chin and snapped it in place, she got a close-up look at his handsome face and those intense green eyes, which reminded her of a deep forest with rays of sunlight streaming through the branches.

When he was confident the helmet fit properly he gave her a nod, lowered the sunglasses from the top of his head, and stepped back. "Go ahead and turn it on."

She'd rather turn *him* on.

But that was a fantasy for another day.

She ran over the procedure in her head and did as he'd instructed, or at least as much as she'd retained. Feeling confident, she looked up at him and gave him a smile as she released the clutch.

The motorcycle jumped out from under her and she ended up ass on the ground.

"Shit." Knees in the dirt, Brady was at her side in a split second. "Are you okay?"

She glanced at the bike lying on its side about ten feet away. "I killed your motorcycle."

"Fuck the bike."

Suddenly his hands were all over her, pulling off the helmet, checking her for injury. Her tailbone hurt and her elbows stung, but other than that she was pretty sure she'd live to see another day. Mostly her pride hurt.

He lifted her arms and checked out the abrasions. They weren't bad. She'd gotten worse the time she decided to try rollerblading at Griffith Park.

"Baby, I'm so sorry." He looked up and their faces were so close she could feel the warmth of his breath on her cheeks. "I guess this wasn't a very good idea."

He'd called her *baby*.

"Will you give me my ten dollars back?"

His eyes searched her face. "Of course."

"Will you bandage me up so we can try it again?"

He smiled. "Absolutely."

She smiled back. "Then you can keep the ten bucks."

"Maybe I should use it to pay for more insurance," he joked as he helped her to her feet.

"Or a six pack of that Shiner stuff you drink." She dusted off her butt. "I could probably use one of those right about now."

"I promise, if you make it through the day, we'll celebrate."

She liked the idea of that.

He kept his arm around her and led her to the tailgate of his truck, as if she were fragile.

"You don't have to help me," she said. "I can walk."

"Maybe I want to help you."

"More of that Southern hospitality stuff?"

He lifted her onto the tailgate, planted his hands on

either side of her hips, and stood between her bare, dusty legs.

"More like maybe I just want an excuse to touch you."

"You do?"

He nodded. "I also want to do this." He cupped her face with his hand, fanned his thumb across her cheek in a long, gentle sweep, and tilted her head up so their eyes met. "Even when I know I shouldn't."

A palpable, sexual tension thickened the air.

Sarah blinked as he lowered his head and lightly brushed his masculine lips across her mouth. He teased with soft, quick kisses before settling in and tasting the seam of her lips. She parted them and invited him in.

With the leisurely, slick glide of his tongue, he devoured her.

Sensation rippled down her spine. Her heart thundered. Her breasts tingled. Her head spun. She clutched his broad shoulders for stability, leaned in, and kissed him back with everything she'd kept bottled up in her soul.

He tasted like cinnamon gum and sexual promise. When he lifted his head, the breathless groan that rumbled in his chest verified he didn't want to stop any more than she did.

"Wow." She sighed. "You kiss really good."

As kisses went, this one was sweet with an undertone that said it could have easily dived into heady waters. Since Sarah had always been an excellent swimmer, she wondered if going back for another dip would be too pushy.

"Sorry." His apology came with a look that defied the word. "I promise not to let that happen again."

Insecurity settled around her heart. "Why not?" Was she that bad?

"Because . . ." He reached behind her and grabbed the first-aid kit from the bed of the truck. Popping open the plastic lid, he pulled out antiseptic wipes and some bandages. He tore open the packages and gently tended to the abrasions on her elbows. "You deserve a guy who isn't damaged goods."

She hadn't had *any* goods, so damaged was fine with her.

"What makes you think you're damaged?" she asked.

"Evidence." He thumped a fist against his chest. "See? Empty."

"Like the tin man?"

He gave a low chuckle. "I suppose."

"Didn't you ever see the end of the movie?"

He tilted his head and the sun caught the gold flecks in his eyes. "Of course."

"Then you know that the tin man only *thought* he didn't have a heart. But it was there all along."

"Sarah?" He pulled the backing from a bandage and placed it over a wound. "I'm not the guy you think I am."

And obviously right now he had no plans for telling her why. Luckily she'd always been patient, and she believed the good things in life were worth waiting for.

Brady was worth waiting for.

"But you *are* the guy who's going to teach me how to ride that stupid motorcycle, right?"

He looked up. "You sure you want to try again?"

She'd taken a risk moving to Texas. No sense putting on the brakes now.

"I may be many things," she said. "But I'm not a quitter."

Chapter Six

ON ANY GIVEN day, Brady would be happy to put on his uniform and get back to work after two days off. His time yesterday with Sarah changed that. Now he longed to have another day he could spend in her company.

As he strapped on his utility belt he thought about how brave she'd been after being dumped off the dirt bike. He admired a woman who charged forward and ignored the bumps along a rocky road. In more ways than one.

She'd finally gotten the hang of easing off the clutch instead of popping it, and side by side, they'd taken off for the hills. His ex would never have gotten on the bike the first time, let alone if she'd hit the ground and needed bandages. Sarah didn't seem to let it bother her. In fact, if the grin she wore while they'd been riding was any indication, she'd enjoyed herself immensely.

When they'd taken a break near the creek, they'd had

a chance to talk. She'd asked him about his family and how it had been growing up on the five-hundred-acre ranch his parents owned. And when she'd learned he was very close to his parents as well as his older sister and younger brother she gave an audible sigh.

He'd learned that particular exhale came from the disadvantages of falling in the middle of a pack of siblings and becoming invisible to her overzealously religious parents. Personally, he didn't understand how she could be overlooked. Not that she was loud and boisterous, but because her sweet nature was rare and special.

By no means did that mean he didn't find her sexy as hell.

She rang the bell so hard on that particular quality he'd had a hard time sleeping after he dropped her off at home. Though he'd managed—with great effort—to refrain from kissing her a second time, he'd always been a man with a creative imagination. Last night, it had worked overtime. This morning when he'd woken up in a tangle of sweaty sheets, he recognized the need to back away from the power of the feelings he was developing.

Quickly.

Sarah wasn't a woman a man should take lightly. She wasn't the type of woman you could have an affair with and then just walk away. She was the kind of woman a man wanted to wake up next to every day. The kind he wanted to make his wife and the mother of his children. The kind whose face he wanted to see as he took his last breath.

Sarah Randall was a forever kind of woman.

He, unfortunately, was not a forever kind of man.

He holstered his Smith and Wesson and walked out onto his porch to grab the newspaper before he headed to the station.

Something crunched beneath his foot.

He looked down.

There beneath the heavy tread of his black tactical boots lay a heart-dotted cellophane wrapper containing a smashed sprinkle-topped fortune cookie.

Damn.

He reached down and swiped it up off the doormat.

Pink, red, and white sprinkles rattled loose inside the cellophane and the little rectangular paper bearing the fortune stuck out from beneath the chocolate coating.

"Good morning."

Brady looked up just as Megan soared by on her bicycle.

"Hey," he yelled. "Hold up a minute."

Megan turned her bike in a 180 and he walked down the path to meet her at the curb.

"What's up?" she asked.

"This." He held up the cellophane. "Megan, I appreciate your efforts but I think I made it pretty clear that we really don't have anything in common."

She folded her arms across the front of her shirt. Beneath the black helmet she scowled. "What the hell are you talking about?"

"This." He held up the cellophane again. "The fortune cookies."

Her brown-eyed gaze locked onto the object in his hand. "You think I've been leaving you gifts?"

He shrugged.

She laughed.

He cringed.

Obviously somewhere he'd lost his law-enforcement skills along with the presumption of innocence.

Judging by the pucker in her highly tweezed brows, Megan was not his secret admirer. Judging by the grimace, she wasn't even in the neighborhood of the idea.

"Obviously I misjudged," he said.

"Obviously."

"I apologize."

"Brady? No offense, but you're wrong. You and I do have something in common. We're both masochists." She put her hands on the handlebars and prepared to take off. "The difference? I only hide behind a mask when I'm wearing leather."

And yep. She went there.

"My suggestion? Get over yourself," she said. "Find a nice little princess to live in that fairy tale you've dreamed up. Or spend the rest of your life alone." She shrugged a shoulder. "Doesn't matter to me. Just seems a waste of a good face, hard body, and real handcuffs."

As she pedaled away, Brady dragged a hand over his face.

Colossal fuckup.

Then again, if Megan hadn't been leaving the cookies, who had?

It could be Ashley even though he wasn't quite nice to her at the diner last week when she'd spilled water all over Sarah. Could be Zena, the second-shift dispatcher down at the station. She flirted with him now and again. Of course, if you listened to the rest of the guys, her sexual preference was questionable. Or maybe it was Lyssa, who'd taken over the Vintage Vogue antique store for her aging mother.

Back to the drawing board.

Maybe today's hidden message would give him some direction.

He tore open the cellophane and pulled out the fortune.

Many people fail because they quit too soon.

Great.

All this mystery and overthinking everything was giving him a giant headache. What he needed was a strong cup of coffee, a little normalcy, and a pretty face to make him feel better.

ON A BUSY morning at Bud's, Sarah was surprised at how much attention two little Band-Aids could garner while you poured someone's coffee. The most creative solution to healing her boo-boos came from Chester Banks, Sweet's oldest, and apparently most amorous, cowboy.

"I promise ya, pretty lady," Chester said. "A couple shots of ol' George Dickel, a little moonlight, and tour of my hayloft'll fix ya right up."

She didn't know any George Dickel, preferred to share a slice of moonlight with a man closer to her own age, and had every intention of staying as far away from Chester's hayloft as possible.

"I appreciate your offer but . . ." She attempted a smile that was friendly but far from encouraging.

"You just call me up when you finish yer shift. I can come pick ya up."

Sarah figured the clicking sound Chester made with his mouth was meant to sound flirtatious, but all it managed to do was dislodge his dentures.

"I'm sorry, sir, that's a violation of ethics code two forty-three."

The deep voice startled her and her head snapped up. Brady stood so close behind her she could feel the heat radiate off his body. His khaki uniform hugged those scrumptious muscles, his cop sunglasses were firmly in place, and a smirk tilted those sensuous lips she'd kissed just yesterday.

Everything from her ponytail to her pink sneakers went into an atomic meltdown.

"Aw, come on." Chester pushed his half-empty coffee cup toward Sarah for a refill. "You and them Wilder boys. I tell ya. Not fair."

"What do you mean, Mr. Banks?" Distracted by the nearness of the hottest guy in town, Sarah overfilled Chester's cup. Dark liquid sloshed over the rim. She quickly wiped it away with the towel in her apron pocket.

"That's Chester to you, pretty lady." Chester gave her a wink with rheumy eyes that sparkled over a nose the size of Mount Rushmore.

Hairless and harmless.

Sarah had met Chester's jovial type before and she decided to tease back.

"That's Sarah to you, Mr. Banks. Now . . ." She leaned a hip against the side of the booth. "You were saying about the good deputy here and those Wilder boys?"

"Always stealing the women," Chester grumbled. " 'Soon as a new one like you comes into town they snatch 'em up. Never give us other guys a chance. His 'code two forty-three' is just another way of sayin' 'back the hell away from my woman.' Ain't that right, Deputy?"

The sudden clarity in the old cowboy's eyes made his sincerity clear. Which begged the question: Did Chester really think he and the cronies at his table had a chance with the younger women in town?

Wait.

What had Chester said?

She turned toward Brady but he was gone. A quick scan of the busy diner pinpointed him on a stool at the counter next to Ben Marshall. Returning her focus back to her job before she foolishly forfeited a way to pay her rent, she took breakfast orders from Chester and his gang then went to refill her coffeepot for the empty cups at the Digging Divas Garden Club table.

Somehow she managed to multitask work and daydreaming. Yesterday's motorcycle adventure with Brady had been fun, scary, and, judging by the scrapes on her elbows, a bit dangerous.

The rewards far outweighed the injuries. Through several lengthy conversations they seemed to have made a real connection. She could tell how much he loved his family. She loved her family too, in a completely different kind of way. Where Brady made it a point to share

Sunday dinners with his family because he truly enjoyed their company, she'd always shown up at family dinners out of duty. She'd never understood the point of being forced to attend an event where the conversation flowed around you, rolling over your head like a great ocean wave that either pulled you further out to sea or completely sucked you under.

For years she'd wondered if the problem had just been her. Recognizing the possibility, she'd made attempts to change the dynamics of her interaction with those who shared her DNA. She'd kept on top of current events, the most popular TV shows and movies, and who was on top in sporting events. After a while it became painfully clear that she could have stood on her head wearing a clown nose and bells on her toes and it would have been for naught. They just weren't interested.

Brady seemed interested.

Not only had he asked about all her favorite things and her life in general, he never missed an opportunity to draw her in and touch her. She remembered those big warm hands on her skin—touching her gently, keeping her safe, and drawing out sensations she was sure she'd only read about in romance novels.

A shot of lust tingled warm in her belly.

With his soft masculine lips he'd given her a devastating kiss.

But only one.

Why?

Now, as she refreshed his coffee he wouldn't meet her eyes. Acted like he hadn't spent the entire day before with his hands on her and his lust-filled eyes touching her intimately.

For some reason Brady kept his passion locked up tight, which, in her eyes, was just a sin. She was sure he had a reason, but she'd never been one to pry into other people's lives. Not even if the curiosity was killing her. Instead she knew she needed to find another way—besides her fortune cookies—to grab his attention. Because as much as she'd like to believe Chester's little comment, she'd always been a realist.

She may not be Brady Bennett's woman now, but that didn't mean the situation couldn't change. She'd just have to work a little harder to get him to come around.

On the other hand, Ben Marshall didn't seem to have a problem looking her square in the eye. He lifted his gaze from the half-eaten stack of buttermilk pancakes on his plate. "How are things going?"

"They're going great. Thanks for asking." Smiling, she tossed a menu and set of silverware down in front of Brady, then turned her attention toward Paige's handsome brother-in-law. "And thanks for your help picking out the right cleats the other day. Hopefully they'll help me hit a home run."

"Let me know if they don't work out. I'd be happy to exchange them for something else. I just got in some new batting gloves too." Ben's ice-blue eyes sparkled with mischief. "Maybe we could discuss them over dinner tonight."

As luck would have it, she didn't miss the glare Brady speared his friend with as he sipped his coffee.

"That does sound like a lot of fun," she said. "But I'm afraid I already have a date."

Brady's head snapped around.

And that's all it took to get those surprise-filled green eyes to meet hers.

Of course, certain people didn't need to know the only *date* she actually had was with a hot bubble bath and catching up on the *Justified* episodes she'd recorded. Because really, if a girl couldn't have a man in the flesh, drooling over Raylan Givens was the next best thing.

"Why am I always a day late?" Ben grumbled.

"I'd be happy to take a rain check if you're still interested," she said, channeling all the bravado Charli had pounded into her yesterday.

"Great." Ben smiled. "How about Friday night?"

"Let me double-check my calendar and get back to you." She turned back to Brady whose hand now seemed to be gripping that coffee cup just a little tighter. "Have you decided what you want?"

"Just coffee." His rough tone said he might be just a little miffed about something.

"You sure?" She stuck her order pad back into the pocket of her apron. "Because I have some delicious treats in the back. Bud made some fresh raspberry scones and blueberry muffins."

His lips were pressed together so tight it didn't surprise her that he gave no response.

It did surprise her that he followed her into the kitchen and out the back door.

"What the hell was that?" he growled.

Jealousy may not look good on some people, but it matched Brady's gorgeous eyes. And it definitely sent a thrill up her spine. She'd never had a guy pay much attention to her, and though Brady vibrated with combustible energy, she didn't feel threatened. She chose to believe all that energy was simply some of his restrained passion trying to push its way out.

How she knew this, she didn't know. Most people would take one look at those narrowed eyes, the shiny badge, and the gun holstered to his hip and run like hell. She'd played it safe long enough. She knew if she trusted her gut, it would lead her in the right direction. Just like the day she'd pointed her car toward Texas.

"Ben seems nice," she said with a shrug.

"He is." The words burst from his mouth in a bitter hiss.

"Then why wouldn't I want to go out with him?" She refrained from batting her eyelashes. Barely.

Confusion and hunger clashed in his eyes like some mythical tempest. His clenched fists flexed the barrel-like biceps exposed beneath the short sleeves of his uniform. His jaw twitched and his gaze dropped to her mouth.

Lust flooded her body in hot, electrically charged waves.

"Why? Because of this." His big hands clasped her arms and dragged her against a wall of hard muscle and heat. His mouth came down and he seduced her with a wild and unrelenting kiss.

Hot and urgent, his tongue swept the recesses of her mouth. She surrendered to his promise of passion, and the ache of her desire.

At barely eight o'clock in the morning Brady had her pinned against the back wall of Bud's Nothing Finer, his thigh pressed between hers, kissing the living daylights out of her. Her bones melted as she wrapped her arms around his neck, clung to him, and kissed him back. Too soon, he was gone and her arms were empty.

She blinked several times to clear the seductive fog he'd lured her into.

"You feel that?" he asked, his voice low, rough, and a little breathless.

"Yeah. I feel it." She dragged her finger up the buttons on his shirt and tapped his stubborn chin. "The question is what are you going to do about it?" Without giving him time to respond she yanked open the screen door and went inside.

An uneven sigh pushed from her lungs as she grabbed the tray containing Bud's scones and muffins and went back out to offer them to diners.

Either she'd just made the biggest fool of herself, or she'd enticed the lion from his den.

Only time would tell.

STUNNED, CONFUSED, AND more turned on than he'd ever been in his life, Brady returned to his seat at the counter. He sipped his now tepid coffee and watched Sarah go on about her day as if they hadn't just locked lips and nearly come apart at the seams.

Around a mouthful of pancake, Ben looked at him and said, "She's not going to go out with me, is she?"

Something hot and possessive stirred in Brady's soul. For the first time in a year, he felt alive.

So what was he going to do? Ignore it because he was too scared to realize a woman like Sarah didn't come around every day? Was he going to let fear keep him from reaching out and taking what he wanted so that she'd end up in someone else's arms?

He regarded the friend next to him. "No way in hell."

Chapter Seven

"You've graduated to the head of the class," Charli said as she came into Sarah's apartment and stuck a cupcake decorated with pink sprinkles in her hand. Pumpkin, Charli's little orange poodle trailed her and immediately went to play with her new BFF, Pilot. "You deserve a treat."

Sarah shut the door and followed her into the living room. "I feel evil."

"Evil! Why would you say that?"

She pointed to the kitchen counter and the newest batch of fortune cookies she'd just finished. "I feel like a stalker. Like I'm setting a trap then sitting back just waiting for him to fall in. I'm not sure I want to *catch* a man that way. What if he wakes up one day and realizes he's been bamboozled?"

Charli perched on a bar stool and gave her a look.

"Don't be ridiculous. We women often have to do something to get them to notice us. Have I mentioned the episode where I told Reno I wasn't wearing panties so he'd get off his fine ass and do something about all the hotness burning between us?"

A laugh bubbled up in Sarah's throat. "That was pretty memorable."

"Yeah, but it woke him up, right? It's not like I tricked him into asking me to marry him. Sometimes they just need a little nudge in our direction. Brady's been a pretty unmovable object since . . ."

"What happened to him to make him that way?"

"It's not my story to tell." Charli sighed. "But I guarantee if *you* get him to tell you about it, that's total confirmation that you've broken the barrier."

"I really like him." Sarah scooted up on the bar stool. "He's not just sexy as heck, he's funny and thoughtful. Plus he carries on a great conversation that isn't just all about him."

"Oh, I so know what you're talking about. I dated guys that couldn't stop talking about themselves. The worst were the gym rats. I swear, if there was a mirror nearby I might as well have stayed home." Charli chuckled. "The opposite happened with Reno. I couldn't get him to talk about himself at all."

Sarah laughed. She liked this new relationship with her former boss. And she was grateful that Charli, with her busy life, found time to nurture the friendship. So far Sarah had no regrets about moving a thousand miles away to Sweet. Not that she was an attention hog, but it was just nice that people actually looked at her, spoke to her, and cared about her opinions.

"Hey," she said. "How did you know anything happened between me and Brady?"

"Because he's sitting at my kitchen table right now, drinking coffee with Reno and asking his advice."

"About?"

Charli's grin spread across her entire face. "You."

"I THOUGHT THE cookies were being left by Megan Walsh." Brady sipped the fresh cup of coffee Reno had just set in front of him. "But when I asked her, she didn't hesitate to let me know I wasn't her type."

"Right." Reno grinned. "Because you're not into the whole whips-and-chains thing."

"You know about that?"

His friend nodded and shuddered. "She came after me there for a while. I swear the dreamy look in her eyes when she mentioned hot wax almost gave me a heart attack. It's nice to have a woman who lights candles to set a romantic mood instead of wanting to drip the residue all over your body."

A twinge tightened Brady's stomach. He didn't get that whole underground world of pain. Thank God. He had enough trouble with matters of the heart. "So how's it going with you and Charli?"

"Thankful for every damn day."

"She really pulled you out of the dark, my friend."

"Exactly. Although there are some days I just want to

bottle up all that effervescence and save it for a rainy day. She wears me out."

"In a good way, right?"

Reno just smiled.

"You're lucky."

"Had to pull my head out of my ass before I lost her." Reno sipped his coffee thoughtfully. "So what do these cookie fortunes say?"

"They're like a bread-crumb trail." Brady grinned. "Trouble is, I have no idea who they're from or where they're leading me. Although I have to admit they've made me curious."

"So you're saying it's a little exciting to have a secret admirer?"

"At first? No. Now? I can't help wonder."

"Eventually she or he will have to reveal themselves, right?"

"*He?*"

Reno shrugged. "You never know."

"I don't swing that way."

"I'm just saying, you never know, and you should be prepared to deal with *whoever* steps up and confesses their undying hotness for you. Obviously they've put a lot of effort into this. Even if it turns out to be someone you might not be interested in, you don't want to crush anyone's feelings."

"Charli's made you soft."

"Actually quite the opposite is true."

"TMI," Brady said even though he barked out a laugh. It always felt good to be around his friends. They made him laugh. And sometimes they just knocked common sense into his thick skull. Texans were known for doing things in a big way. His closest buddies, the Wilder brothers, amped that up times ten.

"Aside from the whole mysterious-cookie thing," Reno said, "there's Sarah."

"Yeah." Just the mention of her name sent his heart racing.

He wanted what his friend had found. He wanted that special someone who completed him. Who'd make him a better man. There had been a time when he thought he'd found her. Looking back now, he'd probably made her up in his head as something she was never meant to be. He just hadn't expected her to be so evil. Or that he'd be dumb enough to be lured into a total fantasy.

Clearly he couldn't trust his gut instincts. Let alone his damn stupid heart. Which explained his complete hesitancy. At least to him.

"And?" Reno asked.

Brady couldn't sort out his feelings quick enough to respond.

Reno jumped in. "A word of advice?"

"That's kind of why I came over."

"Take it from me. I fought leaving my past behind. I was comfortable there, dwelling in the heartache. It became all I knew. And then along came Charli. Eventually I understood that if I didn't reach out and take the hand she offered, I'd be in that dark place for the rest of my life. After a lot of thought I was surprised to realize I was tired of living in the past. I really wanted that 'happily ever after' everyone always talks about. I found it. What's it going to take to convince you?"

"What did it take for you?"

"Fear." Reno gave him a direct look. "I'd lost everything. I figured if I stayed right where I was I wouldn't lose anything ever again. I was wrong. I'd fallen in love with Charli. I just wouldn't admit it. But when I was faced with losing *her*?" He shook his head. "Unimaginable."

In that moment it became apparent to Brady that fear came in many forms.

Reno took a breath and sipped his coffee. Then he gave Brady a look with one eyebrow raised. "Sarah's throwing you a lifeline, my friend. Don't be too afraid or too stupid to grab hold. Give it a chance to see where it can go. You might be surprised."

Until now, Brady had hated surprises. Even sweet ones that came in heart-dotted cellophane wrappers.

He glanced out the kitchen window to the barn and the windows of the apartment above, where Sarah lived.

Maybe it was time for a change.

Chapter Eight

THE FOLLOWING MORNING Brady breathed a sigh of relief as he stepped out onto his front porch and found no heart-dotted cellophane-wrapped fortune cookie.

He blew through the workday with only one deer vs. SUV mishap on Hwy. 46 and a dispute between Patsy Howard and Eleanor Sherman over a secret recipe that had been meant to be kept hush-hush. Eleanor used her bad hearing as an excuse for taking the hundred-year-old formula for funeral casserole to a recipe exchange at the senior center. According to Patsy, her ancestors were turning over in their graves because now everyone on the whole blasted planet knew the hidden ingredient was beer.

Lord have mercy.

He'd come within seconds of cuffing both the elderlies just to shock some sense into their ridiculous blue-haired heads. Lucky for him—and them—they'd come to their senses just in the nick of time. By the time he left them, they were bawling in each other's arms and begging for forgiveness.

When his shift finally ended, he strolled out to his truck to head to the Touch and Go Market for yet another frozen something he could stick in the microwave.

And there it was.

Sitting on top of the hood of his truck was the now familiar heart-dotted cellophane bag bearing the chocolate-dipped, Valentine-colored, sprinkled fortune cookie.

He sighed even as curiosity snuck up on him and bit him in the ass. He looked around the lot to see if there was any evidence of who might have left it. Not a soul was to be found except for the armadillo trotting toward the row of bushes at the back.

Wasting no more time, he tore open the package, cracked open the cookie and read the fortune.

Follow your heart and you will never get lost.

Great.

What if his heart had no fucking clue and he couldn't afford to give it any trust?

SHOPPING AT THE Touch and Go Market proved to be a different adventure from the huge chain markets in Southern California. They had an in-house meat department and the produce always looked fresh and appetizing, but the variety of groceries was limited.

Sarah stood in front of the dry pasta display and tried

to decide whether she wanted the regular or thin variety. Spaghetti had always been one of her favorite meals and since she hadn't heard from Brady in a couple of days, she was in the mood for comfort food. And ice cream. Preferably Blue Bunny's Bunny Tracks. With caramel sauce on top. And a cherry. And maybe a brownie on the side.

"I've never seen anyone bite their lip over pasta decision making before."

The now familiar voice was tinged with humor. Which did nothing to boost her confidence since she'd convinced herself she'd scared him away by asking him such a demanding question. She'd pushed him into a corner. Judging by his disappearing act, he obviously hadn't appreciated her efforts. She'd overstepped her boundaries. While she believed women like Charli had the wherewithal to attract such a man, Sarah had to admit she was drowning.

As of this morning she'd decided to stop trying to be something she wasn't. To stop playing games. She was just plain old Sarah. And all she really wanted to do was find someone to love who would also love her back.

Pretty simple.

Unfortunately, after that kiss behind Bud's Diner and her audacious question, his vanishing act verified Brady either wasn't ready or wasn't interested.

She turned to find him still in uniform, holding a wire hand basket filled with several microwave dinners. She never failed to be awestruck by the way that uniform fit his tall, muscular body, or the way his gold-flecked green eyes made her heart dance. Aside from all the desire his physicality whipped up inside, she was really attracted to the heart he hid behind that shiny badge.

Tomorrow was Valentine's Day. He'd had plenty of time to indicate whether he was interested beyond a stolen kiss behind a diner. He hadn't. And she had to knock down the fairy tale she'd begun to erect.

"Regular spaghetti is more filling than thin," she said, trying to sound nonchalant even though her heart was soaring at rocket speed. "I couldn't decide if I wanted to risk a stomachache or not."

His earnest smile did nothing to slow her racing heart. "Judging by the contents in your basket I assume you're making your sauce from scratch."

"I always do." Mostly because she had too much time on her hands.

He leaned in, bringing with him the seductive scent of warm male. "Why take a chance?" He grabbed a package of thin spaghetti and placed it in her cart.

"Because sometimes it's worth the risk." She retrieved the thin spaghetti from her cart, stuck it back on the shelf, and grabbed a package of regular. After tossing it in her cart, she pushed past him and continued down the aisle.

To her surprise, he followed.

"You mad at me?"

She looked up and melted at the expression of concern on his face. "Why would I be mad?"

"Because I've been avoiding you."

You had to love an honest man.

"Look." Stopping her cart in the middle of the aisle, she sighed. "After that kiss, I asked you what you were going to do. I think you made yourself clear. No reason for me to get upset. I wanted to know. Now I do."

One of the cart's wheels picked up a wad of something off the floor and it the cart wobbled as she pushed it farther down the aisle and away from Brady before she made a fool of herself and started acting all girly. She really liked him. Knowing he didn't feel the same about her? Well, that just plain hurt.

She turned at the end-cap display of baking supplies and bags of Valentine's candy. A sour reminder that once again she'd be spending the holiday of love all alone.

Making a huge attempt to refocus her thoughts on comfort food, she headed toward the produce section. Brady caught her just as she squeezed a tomato to check for ripeness.

"Wait a minute." He moved between her and the vegetables. "You think I'm not interested in you?"

"I don't need to be hit over the head to get it. I got it." She tried to reach past him. "Would you please move aside so I can pick tomatoes for my sauce? Or would you rather wear them?"

A smile flashed across his face.

Why was he smiling?

Did he think hurting her feelings was funny?

His big hands gripped her arms, lifted her to her toes and against his chest. Then he kissed her. Right there between the squash and the hot peppers. Quick. Hard. Possessive.

"I've spent the past two nights without sleep," he said in a rough "I mean business" tone. "Because I couldn't get you off my mind. Does that sound like someone who isn't interested?"

"Well I—"

"Take me home, Sarah. Let's grab a bottle of wine. We can make that spaghetti sauce together, and I'll explain everything."

She didn't know if she wanted to hear *everything*.

But if there was a chance he might kiss her again, how could she say no?

"Okay," she said. "But when it comes to the sauce recipe, it's my way or the highway."

His laughter floated through her heart like a warm mist. "Then lead the way."

Nothing was ever as simple as that. Sarah knew that from experience. But with the intensity he was looking at her with right now, she didn't really care.

BRADY TOOK HER HOME.

To *his* home.

And to *his* kitchen where she looked hot as hell in a very good way.

For the past half hour they'd shared the cutting board. While he chopped onions and garlic per her instructions, she sliced tomatoes, basil, and mushrooms. Along the way she gave him step-by-step directions, and he defied temptation by resisting the need to pull her into his arms and bury his nose in her neck beneath her luxurious cascade of soft ivory hair.

At the moment, with the sleeves of her thin, body-hugging sweater pushed up to her elbows, she stirred another handful of tomatoes into the pot. Brady didn't know exactly why that simple everyday action turned him on so much, it just did.

Before he acted on the caveman instincts that tugged at his groin and insisted he throw her over his shoulder and haul her off to the bedroom, he poured them each a glass of wine. While she stirred the pot, he leaned a hip against the counter and imagined standing behind her with his palms cupped over her breasts as he kissed the back of her graceful neck.

She accepted the glass and took a sip while the savory aroma of the sauce rose from the stove on a puff of steam. Sarah seemed to fit right there in his kitchen. Not because she was a woman cooking a meal for him, but because she made the kitchen come to life. At the same time as he found comfort in her company, she set everything inside him on fire.

He wanted her.

Bad.

But first things first.

"I appreciate this," he said. "It's been a long time since a real meal was cooked in this kitchen."

She looked up at him with those big blue eyes full of curiosity. "How long?"

"A year."

"A year exactly? Or . . ."

"Sarah, I know you're probably used to guys coming on to you fast and hard, but . . ."

She laughed, took a slug from her wine, and promptly

choked. He grabbed a tissue off the counter and handed it to her. While she dabbed at the corners of her eyes he explained, trying not to sound like a total pussy.

"You might have heard I was previously engaged."

"Rest assured your friends have not said a thing to me about your past," she said, stirring the sauce so she didn't have to meet his eyes. "They're loyal to you. And I hate to sound pathetic, but I envy that."

Jesus. She had a family who basically acted like she didn't exist. Now to find out she didn't even have a cluster of friends to help her through all that? He couldn't understand. He felt incredibly lucky to have both friends and family.

She deserved more.

She deserved better.

But was he capable of giving it to her?

He didn't know. And before they went any further she needed to know the truth. To make her decisions based on knowledge, not whatever sexual tension was pulling them together.

"The week before last Valentine's Day my ex-fiancée left romantic notes everywhere about how we were going to spend the holiday." Memories flooded him and threatened to pull him under. "I won't go into details but most were suggestive and peaked my curiosity the week leading up to the big day."

"Did you know your fiancée long before you proposed?"

"Ex. And about six months. She came here from Houston to stay with a sick aunt. When her aunt got better I knew she'd be going back to Houston, so I proposed."

"Did you propose because you loved her? Or just because she'd leave if you didn't?"

He'd asked himself that a million times. He thought he'd loved her. And that was one of the reasons why it was so hard to trust his heart now. "Hard to say now with all the bad feelings she left behind."

"What happened?" Compassion darkened her eyes. If she was half as interested in him as he was her, it wasn't an easy thing to ask.

"We set a date and she moved in here with me. When she started asking a lot of questions, I should have known there was something amiss. But I guess I was blinded by the brightness of the future I pictured in my head."

"What kind of questions?"

"I thought they were typical . . . until later." He shrugged. "Things like how much money I made a year. How far I could go in the department. How big a house I planned to buy her after the wedding. If I expected her to work a full-time job."

"Those sound like normal things that should be discussed before a marriage," she said. "That's why pre-nups were invented. To help clarify that situation."

"You'd think so. But most people go into a marriage because they love each other and want to be together. She had a whole different agenda. On Valentine's Day I came home after work expecting the romantic *surprise* she'd teased me with all week. The surprise was actually me walking through the door and discovering her having sex with Zack Gifford on the kitchen table."

"Oh my God." Her hands went to her mouth. Her eyes widened. "Are you serious?"

"Unfortunately."

"*That* kitchen table?"

"Hell no. I took that piece of trash out and burned it."

"No wonder you looked like you wanted to murder Zack the night we played pool at Seven Devils."

"I've always been taught to take the high road." He inhaled a breath of air to clear the residual ache the breakup left behind. "Besides, murder was too good for him. Or her."

"How could she do something like that? That's just . . ."

"Evil?"

"Yeah."

"My thoughts exactly. Little did I know she'd just been looking for some love-stricken idiot to take care of her for the rest of her life in the manner she thought she deserved. After I threw Zack out the door—"

"Physically?"

"Oh yeah."

"Good for you."

He wanted to be able to laugh, but the memory was still too raw. "She tried to justify her actions by saying she didn't know any other way to let me know she didn't want to marry me. She said both me and my job were too dangerous." Agitated, he shoved his hands onto his hips. "I've never laid a hand on anyone. And around here I'm more likely to get run over by a herd of goats than taken down by any kind of criminal behavior. At the end of the day, it hadn't been the danger associated with me or my job she was worried about. It had been—in her opinion—the insignificant paycheck that came with the uniform."

Sarah snagged her bottom lip between her teeth and shook her head. "I don't understand why she would do something so mean. Why not just tell you she couldn't marry you? You're a reasonable man." Her lips curved in a little smile. "Most of the time anyway."

"I do have my moments."

"Where is she now?"

"Married to a second-string linebacker on the Houston Stallions."

"I imagine he can probably fend for himself."

"She's got pretty sharp claws." He shrugged, feeling relief that his ex had actually pulled such a vicious stunt. He couldn't imagine being married to her and having a couple of kids only to discover her true self. "I just thought you should know what's held me back."

Beneath the bright overhead light, a pink flush crept up her cheeks. "I appreciate your honesty."

Any woman in her right mind would run like hell right now. He waited for Sarah to pick up her purse and bail out the door.

To his surprise, she didn't.

"It's not that I'm not interested," he further explained, feeling like he was throwing daggers or at the very least using the pathetic "It's not you, it's me" speech. "It's just that I'm not a forever kind of guy. I can't make—"

"Promises," she said. "I get it. Warning received." Her blue eyes searched his face and her expression stayed neutral. "And denied."

Chapter Nine

SARAH KNEW SHE couldn't change Brady's past. All she could do was try to lead him into the future. Whatever this was between them—just sex, friendship, or a possibility for love—she wanted to connect with him on a level that mended the dark moment in his life that made him wary as a black cat on Halloween.

For most of the world Valentine's Day was a day to celebrate love, hope, and romance. For the rest it was a horrible reminder that you were alone, unwanted, unloved.

For Brady the day represented failure, heartache, and loss.

"You don't honestly believe you had anything to do with her actions, do you?" The look on his face was killing her. She'd never seen such a combination of defeat and embarrassment wrestling for dominance. "You're an incredible man, Brady Bennett. Don't you judge yourself harshly because she's a . . ."

A smile curled his mouth. "A what?"

"Well, I don't usually cuss, but she's just a . . . beeotch. And you can't spend the rest of your life feeling bad about what happened. Be thankful you discovered her true colors before you actually signed a marriage license."

"I *am* thankful."

"But you're not done beating yourself up. And you're still afraid to trust anyone."

"You're right. I don't trust easily anymore."

As much as Sarah had always despised the loneliness of the hearts-and-flowers holiday, she wanted to make sure Brady knew he hadn't failed. And that any woman he chose to be a part of his life would be lucky beyond anything she could imagine.

She knew she should come clean right now. Be honest that she was the secret admirer who'd left him daily reminders of the worst day of his life. His ex's deceit had been meant to cause harm. Sarah's motive had strictly been affection. Though she feared he might see it differently. And that was what prevented her from telling him the truth. She was afraid he would push her away. Step back from the bond that had been growing between them since that morning at the diner.

"Don't let her do that to you, Brady."

There was no need for her to channel the bad girl she thought he might find appealing. All she needed to do was go with her heart and hope to heck it didn't get broken.

In another colossal leap of faith, she pulled on her wings and jumped.

With a yearning to ease the sting his ex had left behind, Sarah set the burner beneath the Dutch oven containing the spaghetti sauce on simmer and turned toward the man for whom she'd developed intense feelings. Not to mention a whole lot of white-hot desire.

"By the way," she said. "You never answered my question."

"I'm sorry." The frown that curled his dark brows made him look vulnerable—a rare slip of control for such a strong man. "Which one?"

She pushed away from the counter and moved toward him, close enough to feel the heat from his body. Her head got dizzy as she breathed him in and wrapped her fingers in the front of his shirt. As she pulled him down, she lifted to her toes and pressed her parted lips softly to his.

In much less of a hurried encounter than the kiss they shared at the Touch and Go, Sarah teased him with the promise of something hotter. He tasted sweet like wine as their tongues touched and swirled. In one swift motion his arms wrapped around her. His hands glided down the curve of her back then cupped her bottom in a hungry caress. In response, her nipples hardened and peaked against his chest. He gave an appreciative groan that sent shivers up her legs and into her lady parts.

Then she pulled her head back just enough to be able to look him in the eye and ask the question he'd voiced behind the diner. "Feel that?"

He gave a slow nod.

"So . . ." She kissed him again, snagged his bottom lip between her teeth, then soothed the flesh with her tongue. Then she repeated her own question. "What are you going to do about it?"

The deep timber of his voice rumbled against her chest. "Baby, right now I'll do whatever you want."

"Then take me to bed." Somewhere along the way shy Sarah had completely dissolved into the Sarah who really needed this man. She wanted his heart too, but for now, she'd take what she could get. Hopefully she'd have time to work on the rest later.

Tingles settled low in her abdomen as his hand slipped around her waist and drew her against him. His erection pressed against her as his hot mouth found the sensitive curve of her neck.

"Whatever the lady wants," he said against her skin. Then he lifted her into his arms and carried her down the hall and into his room as if she weighed less than a feather.

When he set her on her feet his lips brushed over hers and he tenderly kissed her. Her heart thundered in her ears as his firm, determined mouth coaxed and teased and the kiss turned into something she'd only dreamed.

"I might not be very good at this," she whispered. "Don't be disappointed."

He leaned back and looked at her. "The only way you could disappoint me is if you'd walk out the door right now."

"There's no chance of that happening."

"I'm glad." He kissed her again. "And I have a confession to make. I haven't done this in such a long time I might not be very good either. So maybe we can just figure things out as we go along."

She couldn't imagine he'd be bad at anything. Especially making love. He had a body built for sex. And when his slick, hot, hungry tongue slipped inside her mouth she dove into the dizzying pleasure that stirred up from the heat of her core and into the swollen peaks of her breasts.

Strong fingers plunged into her hair and she clung to him while his mouth made her crave more, more, more. He wrapped his arms around her and brought her firmly against him. His long, thick erection pressed into the junction of her thighs and plunged her into a pool of white-hot passion and need.

His fingers slipped up her side, snuck beneath her sweater, and caressed her breast. As his thumb brushed across her nipple in a lazy motion, she leaned into him. The musky scent of his male arousal filled her senses. She wanted to wrap her legs around him and let him sweep her away in a sea of sensation.

"I want to see you naked," he whispered in a voice roughened by lust.

"Me too." Her fingers got busy undoing the buttons on his uniform while he pulled her sweater over her head. When his khaki shirt sailed to the floor, she slid her hands down his warm chest to his flat, muscled belly. "God, you look even better without clothes."

Eyes bright, he smiled. "My turn." He released the clasp on her bra and tossed it aside. Then those intense eyes just looked at her. The more he looked, the more desperate she became to feel the heat of him surrounding her and filling her deep inside.

Their boots and pants went next. Sarah expected to feel embarrassed, but the way he looked at her made her feel like a rare treasure. She'd never had a man look at her the way he did. It was like a drug to her system. A balm to her heart.

"That morning at the diner, I had no idea how beautiful you were." He smoothed his palms down the curves of her body. "Inside and out."

He drew her against him. When their bare flesh met, she melted. The silky texture of the light covering of hair on his chest tickled and teased her erect nipples. His moist mouth skimmed her neck, kissed the curve of her shoulder, then moved lower. He licked his tongue over her nipple before he drew the sensitive bud into the hot recess of his mouth.

Eyes closed, her head dropped back. He held her by her waist while he licked and suckled. Every delicious pull of his mouth sent a ripple of pleasure straight to her core.

"I want to touch you," she whispered. Her eager fingers slid down his warm, rippled belly and curled over his substantial erection. She stroked the smooth, hard length. Tested the weight of his testicles. And smiled when he moaned and pushed himself into her hand.

"I can't wait any longer," he murmured against the side of her throat while his roughened fingertips toyed with her sensitive nipples. His teeth nipped her earlobe and his warm breath brushed her cheek.

"Me either." Her words escaped on a rush of air.

He eased her to the bed and followed her down. He looked into her eyes. "Are you sure about this?"

"I've never been more sure of anything in my life."

"Mmmm." He fed her deep, wet kisses. Rocked his hips forward until the plump head of his penis nudged and teased her slick opening.

A moan of pure pleasure and need vibrated in her throat. "Now. Please."

For a moment he pulled away and she mourned the loss of his heat and touch as he tore open a foil packet and rolled on a condom. Then he was back, grinning down at her.

"You were gone so long," she said.

"I promise to make up for lost time." He kissed her, soft and tender as he parted her legs and moved between them.

Anticipation quickened in her chest. When he slid into her body, it was as if he was meant to be there. He filled her completely. He withdrew, and with a long groan, plunged into her again. Deeper than before. With an in and out motion he touched all the amazing places inside her body she never knew existed. His thrusts alternated between slow and fast, short and long. His hips rotated and suddenly her entire universe became him and where their bodies were joined.

She wrapped her legs around him and held him close

while she rode the intense coils of pleasure that licked at her core. Her heart beat erratically in her ears. His breath whispered across her temple as he increased the rhythm. Then he reached between their bodies and touched her swollen, throbbing flesh. He rubbed his thumb over the tip and she nearly burst out of her skin.

"Come for me, baby." His throat was clogged with passion. "I want to watch you completely let go."

His fingers moved faster as he pounded into her body. She felt the first consuming wave of intense sensations that started at her toes and flashed like fire across her skin into her pulsating core. Tremor after tremor rippled across her flesh and stole her breath. Her muscles contracted and gripped him tight deep inside. As a wave of delicious release rolled her into oblivion, she cried out his name.

BRADY ALLOWED HIMSELF total freedom while he made love to Sarah. Each deep thrust inside her body brought him closer to her heart. The more she moaned, the more he wanted to give. Sensation didn't just run through the core of his cock, it touched every pulse point in his body. When her breathing increased and she cried out his name, her climax gripped him a place deep inside he hadn't allowed anyone to touch for a very long time.

And it felt damned good.

Pleasure looked good on her. And he wanted to make sure he could see that relaxed smile on her face more often.

He pushed harder and faster, reaching for that storm of sensation and flash of heat. At last, with a long groan of pleasure, he thrust into her one last time, allowing the fire to consume him.

Together their hearts beat wildly, until gradually their breathing eased. When Sarah let go a long, satisfied sigh he rolled to his side and tucked her into his arms. With her nestled contentedly against him, he now knew his response to her question, What was he going to do about it?

SARAH HAD NEVER felt like she belonged anywhere. But as Brady cuddled her in his arms, she felt like she'd finally come home. His long, contented sigh hinted he might be feeling the same.

Her eyes drifted shut as she enjoyed his warmth and the solid security of his body pressed close. Contentment and the slow and steady beat of his heart lulled her toward slumber. Every muscle, every pore in her body relaxed.

Brady sighed again.

This time it came with a declaration.

"I trust you, Sarah."

Sarah's eyes popped open.

She knew she should tell him right now that she was his secret admirer. Heck, she should have told him before she took off her clothes.

For a moment she lay there, heart pounding with worry.

Tell him.

Tell him.

Tell him.

She opened her mouth to do just that. Then he kissed her shoulder, kissed her neck, and his big hand slid up her stomach to caress her breast. He came to life again, pressing his erection against her backside while his magic fingers slipped between her legs. In that moment when she should have stopped what was happening and admitted her secret, she turned in his embrace, and tumbled into the passion darkening his eyes.

With absolute selfish need, she took him in her hand and kissed him back.

Tomorrow she would tell him the truth, she promised. Tonight she just wanted to be the woman in his arms. The woman he trusted.

Even if tomorrow that belief shattered like broken glass.

Chapter Ten

MORNING AFTERS OFTEN came with regret.

Sarah couldn't face that reality.

Not yet.

Quiet as a mouse, she slipped from Brady's embrace and his bed. She grabbed her clothes up off the floor and darted into the bathroom to dress before she rushed out of his house. Tomorrow had come and she no more had the courage to face her deception in the light of day than she had in the dark of night.

Darn her foolish, cowardly heart.

Dawn barely lit the sky as she closed his front door and jumped into her Escape. Though they'd gotten up after their second round of making love to eat the spaghetti they'd prepared earlier, her stomach growled. She'd never had such a vigorous workout. Round two had turned into a passionate round three and then some. And she'd still not found the courage to tell him.

For years she'd dreamed and imagined what it would be like to be made love to by a man who not only knew what he was doing, but who also put his whole heart into it. Brady did just that. And if last night became the only night she experienced such passion, she'd have enough memories for a lifetime.

Now what to do?

Today was the cursed Valentine's Day.

With good reason, Brady had made it clear he despised the holiday. She imagined he'd do his best to carry on and ignore all the hearts-and-flowers hoopla like it was any other day. With all he'd been through on this particular holiday, the last thing she wanted was to add to his troubles. But the turmoil in her conscience and the ache in her heart warned her that the payment for her dishonesty was past due.

He'd never mentioned the mysterious cookie deliveries, but after hearing him recount the disastrous way he discovered the ugly hidden agenda of the woman he'd planned to marry, she understood why.

Brady hated surprises.

And she couldn't blame him.

What she had intended as a fun way to grab his interest had soured because of his past. Still, her own duplicity didn't bode well for the start of a new relationship.

If there was even the possibility of one once she'd admitted the truth.

THE SAPPY HOLIDAY of hearts and flowers seemed to have been set up as a bitter reminder of all that Brady had lost. Waking up in bed alone after holding Sarah all night put the cap on it.

Why did she run?

Maybe he hadn't lived up to her expectations. Maybe he should have kept the story of what had happened with his ex private. A million more *maybes*—each one more ridiculous than the next—drilled through his head as he took a shower and got ready for work.

He thought about the *Valentines Day Most Wanted* newspaper article and the qualities he said he looked for in a woman. No one fit that description better than Sarah.

Though she might not see herself as such, she was confident enough to move a thousand miles away from everyone and everything she knew. She was adventurous enough to climb on a motorcycle and risk injury. She could have easily whipped his ass in pool had she not held back. She cooked like a master chef. And she certainly set him on fire. Most of all she made him want to reach for the stars and be a better man.

He trusted her.

Who could ask for more?

Yet today she'd disappeared like morning fog. No good-bye. No note. Not a single sign existed that she'd even been there except rumpled sheets and a lingering hint of her sweet scent.

As he turned on the coffeemaker, he pulled out his

phone to call her and realized he didn't have her phone number.

One more piece of the Sarah puzzle to solve.

AN ADDED BENEFIT to renting the apartment space above Reno Wilder's barn was you had access to miles of rolling hills and scenic landscape. All the better to mosey, ponder, and delay. Warm sunshine beat down on Sarah's back as she took a hike that lasted for hours. Never having been in a relationship that lasted more than a blink, and never having been in a situation like the one she'd currently landed in, she'd needed time to clear her thoughts and conquer the nerves holding her back from telling the truth.

Reno's lively Australian shepherd, Bear, accompanied her and made her grateful she'd left her cell phone behind. Otherwise she might have been too distracted to sidestep the scorpion who'd come out of his hole. Or view the majestic hawk circling overhead. Or barely notice the deer before they sprang away.

By the time she got back to the apartment it was late afternoon. When she picked her phone up off the counter she saw several missed calls from Brady. No texts. No voice mails. Apparently he'd cared enough to have gotten her phone number from Paige or Charli.

Her stomach tightened.

She'd run all day from the facts. Though it would be easier to call him back and reveal herself so she didn't have to witness his disappointment or anger, in her heart, she knew what must be done.

And it needed to be done in person.

SARAH PARKED ON the street in front of Brady's house. She took a deep breath for courage, got out of the car, and walked up to his front door. The lights were on so she hoped he was home.

Lightly she knocked on the door, stepped back, and took another breath.

When the door opened, Brady stood there with his arms full of wine, chocolates, and a beautiful bouquet of red and pink roses.

"Sarah." Surprise flashed. "I was just on my way—"

"I'm sorry." She interrupted him, not wanting to hear where he was going or who those flowers might be for. How she managed to speak past her racing heart and emotion-clogged throat was nothing short of a miracle. "I don't usually just barge in on people. Especially on holidays. But after what you told me last night I knew I had to confess."

"Confess?" His brows pulled together. "Sounds serious."

"Last night you said you trusted me. But . . . I haven't been completely honest." She fought the urge to hang her head. "I know you have a problem with Valentine's Day— with good reason—but I didn't know that before. And I thought it was time you knew."

"Knew what?"

She opened her purse, removed the heart-dotted cellophane-wrapped fortune cookie, and held it up. "I'm the one who's been leaving these for you. I'm sorry. I know you don't like surprises."

"You're the one?" The tone in his voice gave nothing away.

She nodded. "I should have said something last night before . . ." Sadness engulfed her and she sighed. "Well . . . I just thought you should know." Unable to face the disappointment on his face or the ache in her heart, she turned to leave.

His hand shot out and caught her by the wrist. "Wait a minute."

As he forced her to turn around, she squeezed her eyes shut.

"Sarah. Look at me."

She shook her head.

"Why?"

"I don't want to see the look in your eye when you realize everything you see about me is a façade. I'm not the woman you think I am. It's all been stuff I asked to learn from Charli and Paige because I'm not all that exciting. I just wanted . . ." Why did confessions have to hurt so much? "I just wanted you to maybe notice me."

He tugged her closer, tucked his fingers beneath her chin, and tilted her head. "Open your eyes, Sarah."

Only the gentleness in his voice convinced her to do so.

"I see you, Sarah. *You.* Not the flirt you tried to be.

Although that was fun. I see a courageous woman with a generous heart who makes me want to be a better man."

"But I thought—"

"You changed everything," he said. "I'm tired of dwelling on what once was. I'd rather focus on what can be. I want to be with you."

"I want to be with you too."

A smile lit up his face and the genuine warmth of it flowed into her heart.

"I was just on my way to your apartment." He held up the flowers, wine, and chocolates and gave her a megawatt smile. "These are for you, baby. Happy Valentine's Day."

Deliriously happy tears flooded her eyes. To know that somehow she'd been able to turn a horrible holiday he wanted to ignore into one he was willing to celebrate split her heart wide open with love. Maybe neither of them was ready to say the words yet, but they were definitely on the right path.

His kiss was soft and tender and full of promise.

"Happy Valentine's Day." While she took his gifts and held them close to her heart, he took the cookie she'd made just for him in his big, wonderful hands.

With a leaping heart she watched him tear open the cellophane wrapper, break open the cookie, and read the fortune that said

In dreams and in love there are no impossibilities.

"Thank you." He looked at her and smiled. "For opening my eyes. And my heart."

The gifts between them were squished when he took her in his arms and kissed her.

When they finally managed to ease apart she said, "So you don't mind that I'm your secret admirer?"

He held her in his arms and pressed his forehead to hers. "All this time, I hoped it was you."

For most people it took a life-changing event to realize one needed to make changes.

For Sarah Randall, happiness started with a cookie.

**Enjoy *Sweet Fortune*?
Don't miss the rest of Candis Terry's
sparkling, sexy Sweet, Texas, series . . .**

ANYTHING BUT SWEET
Book 1

If Charlotte Brooks thinks she and her TV make-over show can turn Reno Wilder's hometown upside down, he'll be happy to prove her wrong. The ex-Marine has seen too much turmoil and he likes Sweet just the way it is. Traditional. Familiar. A little dull. Everything Charli *isn't*. But instead of backing off from his scowls like everyone else, Charli digs in her skyscraper heels.

Reno Wilder is a one-man *un*welcoming committee, but Charli isn't budging. It's clear the gorgeous cowboy needs an overhaul just as much as Sweet. Someone needs to break him out of that gruff shell and show him how fun and rewarding a little change can be.

Available now!

SWEETEST MISTAKE
Book 2

Firefighter and former Marine Jackson Wilder has "tough guy" down to an art, but he's learned the hard way that promises were made to be broken. Abigail Morgan had once been his best friend, his first kiss, his first love, his first everything. He'd just forgotten to mention all that to her and she blew out of his life. Five years later, she's back and he's battling a load of mistrust for her disappearing act. But for some reason he just can't keep his lips—or his hands—to himself.

When her stint as a trophy wife abruptly ends, Abby returns home to Sweet, Texas, and comes face-to-face with Jackson—her biggest and sexiest mistake. Time and distance did nothing to squash her love for the act-first-think-later stubborn hunk of a man, and when he suggests they renew their old just-friends vow, Abby realizes she wants more. She'd cut and run once. Could she do it again? Or could she tempt him enough to break his promise?

Available now!

SOMETHING SWEETER
Book 3

Seattle event planner Allison Lane is an expert at delivering the perfect wedding—even if she might not exactly believe in the whole "till death do us part" thing. When her father decides to tie the knot with a woman he barely knows, Allison heads to Sweet, Texas, to make sure his new honey is the real deal. What she didn't expect to find at the local honky-tonk was a sexy Southern man as bent on charming her pants off as he is blowing her "true love doesn't exist" theory all to hell.

Veterinarian, former Marine, and Sweet's favorite playboy Jesse Wilder takes one look at Allison and knows she's a handful of trouble he can't deny. But even after a sizzling kiss and obvious mutual attraction, it seems Allison has no such problem. When Jesse uncovers her sweet side, can he crush his playboy image, melt her cynical heart, and change her mind about taking a trip down the aisle?

Coming Summer 2014!

MAJOR LEAGUE CRUSH

Jennifer Seasons

To Breana,
because you know, and still love,
the real Ambush Predator.

Chapter One

BERTIE COGSWELL.

It was a horrible name and she knew it. But, it wasn't nearly as awful as her full name, Roberta Doyle Francine Cogswell. In third grade, she'd gotten tired of being called every variation of Robert and shortened her name to just plain Bertie. And that had improved things some, until the zipper disaster of junior year earned her the unflattering nickname Dirty Bertie. After that she pretty much gave up trying to rise above it and just succumbed to her lot in life as an average woman with an ugly name.

Still, she hated introducing herself. Maybe she'd forgo introductions at the singles pre-Valentine's party her best friend was making her attend tonight and see how that went. Just skip the whole name-introducing thing altogether. She'd probably spend the whole night sitting alone, but that's okay. Valentine's Day annoyed her anyway. Scoring a date for it wasn't high on her priority list.

Bad name aside, it's not like the rest of her was all that much better anyway, Bertie thought as she moved through her kitchen, searching for her coffee bean grinder. A social outcast all of her life, even college hadn't proven to be her time to bloom. Instead she'd hidden out in her dorm room or the library, dust and books her truest friends. They never criticized. And they certainly didn't make fun of her for still being a virgin at twenty like her roommate Christy had. They did help her graduate summa cum laude, though.

Take that, Christy the Slut.

After college she'd worked at a few smaller newspapers doing grunt work until the senior editor at the *Denver Post* had caught her doodling in a sketch pad during lunch hour. Harold had laughed so hard over what she'd drawn, he'd dislodged his toupee and popped a button on the front of his shirt. No joke. Then he'd given her a spot in the Sunday comics and her strip *F@#$MY LIFE*, about a socially awkward, ordinary girl trying to make it on her own in the big city while searching for Mr. Right, had been born.

Now it was syndicated and appeared in many papers across the U.S. and one Canadian magazine. Which was great for her. It afforded her a nice lifestyle and allowed her to work from home.

Professionally successful she was. Personally, not so much. Other than a few Internet dating fiascos, Bertie had really only ever had one relationship, which had ended abruptly when she'd walked into her bedroom one day and found the boyfriend trying on her underwear.

Word on the street was, Larry now went by Larissa and performed on Saturday nights at the Snake Lounge to the immortal words of Chaka Khan. Probably in Bertie's underwear, too, the creep.

A thump sounded at her front door, distracting her from the all-important job of grinding coffee. Bertie looked at the clock on her microwave and noted it wasn't even six A.M. yet. That must be the paper, she thought as she smothered a yawn and shoved a clump of frizzy hair out of her eyes. The latest addition to her strip would be in there, paying homage to Valentine's Day, Bertie-style.

Dumping the grounds into her coffeemaker, she hit the power switch and smiled to herself. Her alter-ego character, Bonnie, was deeply obsessed with the professional baseball player who lived across the hall from her. In the comic, Bonnie had pulled out all the stops to impress him this week as his secret Valentine. The strip ended with her perched on the top of a building across the street like a gargoyle with a ginormous pair of binoculars aimed at his living-room window. She was waiting to see his reaction when the singing telegram and fifty pounds of heart-shaped chocolates with his face imprinted on them were delivered. Poor guy had no idea who his secret admirer was, either.

Kind of like Drake Paulson, the real-life ballplayer who lived across the hall from Bertie.

Not that she was crazy or obsessed. That was all Bonnie. God, she wouldn't have the nerve even if she was a quack. Still, Drake was everything she'd ever wanted in a man. She watched the Rush's games. She knew all about him, all about his crazy antics on and off the field. It was what she liked so much. The guy had this huge, magnetic personality. He just embraced who he was to the fullest and had fun with it. She wished she could be like that. Wished she could have the confidence to paint herself green and dress up like the Jolly Green Giant, like he had for last Halloween. When she'd passed him in the hallway wearing that costume all she'd been able to do was stare. His confidence and comfort in his own skin were the sexiest things she'd ever seen.

For the past two years they'd been living across from each other. And over that time, Bertie had seen her fair share of bimbos and trollops come and go from his place. Not once had she seen anyone remotely normal, or dare she say, *average*. Not that she could really blame him for the type he obviously preferred. He was the first baseman for the Denver Rush—a famous, adored-by-the-public, richer-than-God athlete. Of course he went for those types of women.

Still, to quote a line from her favorite TV character, Liz Lemon, she wanted to go to there.

"In your dreams, Bertie," she muttered to herself and poured a cup of steaming coffee.

Padding to the door in her Nick-and-Nora flannel pajamas, cup in hand, Bertie felt a quick jolt of anticipation. What if she saw him when she opened the door? What if he was right there? What would she say to him?

Probably something eloquent, like, "*Err.*"

Kicking a pair of Nikes out of the way, Bertie reached the front door and craned up onto her tippy toes before she could look quickly through her peephole. Grumbling, she adjusted her glasses and peered through. Nothing. The hallway was completely empty. No sign of the ballplayer anywhere.

Okay, so maybe she was also blessed with a whole lot of shortness. She liked to think what she lacked in the perpendicular, she made up for with her sparkling wit and killer one-liners. Who needed height when they had an irresistible personality anyway?

Anybody who's had to grab a chair to reach a can of soup that was placed on the top shelf of the cupboard, that's who.

Telling herself it was for the best, Bertie slung the door wide and stepped into the hall to retrieve her newspaper. Just as she bent down the grab it, the door across the hall opened. Jolting upright, she sloshed coffee over the rim of her mug and drenched the front of her shirt, scalding her chest.

"Damn it!" Forgetting who was standing only a few feet away as pain assailed her, Bertie ripped open the front of her pajama top and began blowing on the angry red burn. "Ooh, it hurts!" she cried softly, tears stinging her eyes.

Too busy fanning herself with her free hand to hear the door close, she was shocked when a cold washcloth was shoved under her nose a few seconds later. "Here, girlie. Put this on it."

The deep rumble had her head whipping up. When

she spotted Drake towering over her barely a foot away, every ounce of intelligence leaked out her ears and all she said was, "Fart." Just because she'd had a brain fart didn't mean she had to say it out loud! *Ugh*. Stupid mouth.

His eyebrows nearly shot up into the curly brown hair on his head. "Come again?"

Mortification swept through her and had her voice going squeaky. "Bart! Your name is Bart, right?"

The huge ballplayer chuckled and shook his head. "Ahh." The way his rich brown eyes sparked with humor told her that he wasn't fooled. "Nope, name's Drake Paulson."

A slow smile spread across his face, and her heart got all floppy. When he grinned, his whole face changed. It lit up and turned his ordinary features amazing. He had the kind of looks that were gruff and rugged—all raw-boned and manly. There was nothing soft about the guy. Not even his hair, which sprang up in tight brown curls all over his head. She imagined if she pushed on them they'd just pop right back up like a coil.

Was it wrong that she'd fantasized about doing just that on more than one occasion?

Ugh! Maybe she was just as bad as her alter-ego. Where else would Bonnie even learn to do half that crazy stuff?

Feeling down on herself, Bertie grabbed the washcloth from Drake and mumbled without making eye contact, "Thanks."

One of his large hands came into view as he waved it at her. "Your, um, *you knows* are showing."

She wasn't sure, but she thought his voice sounded a little weird—like he had a frog in it.

Suddenly his words registered and she looked down, gasping at the sight. "Oh my God!" Her button-up pajama top was flung wide open and her "you knows" were indeed on full display. Heat flooded her cheeks. It just figured she would be wearing her oldest bra—the one with the frayed hems and busted out underwire.

Welcome to Bertie Cogswell. Take a seat, everyone, and enjoy the show. One of these days she'd really love to make it just twenty-four hours without humiliating herself. Please?

Good Lord, she couldn't even close her shirt because both hands were full.

"Here, let me help."

Before she could emit a squeak of protest, Drake reached out and buttoned her back up, his movements sure and no-nonsense. Then he grabbed her hand with the washcloth that had gone limp at her side and repositioned it over her still-stinging burn. The cold on her tender skin was a welcome relief.

Unsure what to do next, Bertie snuck a peek up at him through her shaggy bangs only to find him smiling gently at her. "Thanks."

"Anytime."

He turned to go, making her stomach pitch with disappointment. Before she could think better of it she stepped toward him. "Wait."

Drake looked back, clearly amused. "Yeah?"

Stumped, Bertie scrambled for something to say. She wasn't even sure why she'd stopped him to begin with, outside the fact that she was pathetically infatuated with him. Maybe that was reason enough.

Think, brain, think. "You forgot your washcloth."

All she heard in return was *wha-wha-wha-wha*, like Charlie Brown's teacher, because she was too busy getting lost in his deep brown eyes. They were the color of mahogany.

"I'm sorry. What?"

Laughter rumbled in his chest, low and steady like a diesel engine. "I said to keep it, little mouse."

She scrunched her nose at that. Just because she was kind of a mousy person didn't mean she wanted to be reminded. But before she could take further offense, he pointed to her feet, which were covered in mouse slippers, and said, "Smooth your feathers, girlie. I'm digging the footwear."

Really?

He liked her dorky slippers? Opening her mouth, Bertie closed it again, feeling completely stymied. It made no sense to her at all why somebody like him would like fuzzy mouse slippers. He was awesome sauce.

"Oh." It was literally the only thing she could think to say. Damn she was smooth.

Drake bent down to retrieve the newspaper in front of his door, the navy blue gym shorts riding up the back of his thick well-sculpted thighs. Bertie inwardly sighed at the sight of his muscular hamstrings on display. Yeah, she definitely wanted to go to there.

Then *hallelujah*, an actual a thought occurred to her. "You get the newspaper." She never said it was an intelligent thought.

Straightening to his impressively full height, he smoothed the front of his faded gray Rush T-shirt and replied, "Only for the comics."

Her heart stopped.

Her comic strip was in there. Forgetting all about the coffee burn, Bertie blurted, "Which ones do you like?"

Drake scratched his scruffy chin, clearly considering. "Well, I gotta say I'm partial to that girlie comic. You know, that one with the crazy girl in love with the ballplayer? The one where she's always wooing him with presents? That shit's funny."

All she could do was nod. Her throat had closed up tight. He thought she was funny.

She could die happy right now.

"What about you?" he asked as he gestured to her own paper. "Which one do you like?"

Swallowing hard around the constriction in her throat, she rasped, "The same."

Drake flashed a grin at her that was both playful and sexy as hell. "You got a thing for ballplayers too, eh?"

If only he knew.

The fact was, she had it bad for a particular ballplayer and absolutely no courage, so she'd been living vicariously through Bonnie for the past two years. Her alter ego had so much courage, she was like an ambush predator, always cornering the poor hapless baseball star in every compromising position possible. All in the name of love.

It was hilarious on paper.

In real life it was just, well, sad. She spent her time pining for something that was never going to happen. Drake Paulson was way out of her league.

"Hey, what's your name again?"

"Why?" Bertie looked up in surprise.

"Your name's Why?"

She shook her head. "No, why do you ask?" They'd lived across from each other for two years and he hadn't once asked in all that time.

"Because we're neighbors."

Oh. Great. He was just being polite.

But something flickered in his eyes when he added, "And because I like you, little mouse. You're interesting."

Kill her dead. Now. "It's Bertie," she whispered. She was surprised she hadn't shouted. Every cell inside of her was jumping up and down for joy.

The man of her dreams liked her. He actually *liked* her.

"What do you do for a living, Bertie?" He looked at her like he was actually interested in the answer.

She eyed the paper and felt her cheeks flame. "I'm a comic-strip artist."

His eyebrows shot up. "No shit? You mean like this?" He held up the paper and wiggled it.

It was amazing she could speak. "Yeah, something like that." If he asked any more questions she might just faint. How mortifying it would be if he found out she was Roberta C and about her huge crush on him! She'd never be able to look at him again. God, she'd have to move. Maybe to a new country.

Drake placed a hand on his doorknob and twisted, saying, "That's hella cool. See you around then, Bertie." He took a step inside and then turned back to her. "Hey, you hitting up Geoff's party tonight on the tenth floor?"

She nodded, hugely relieved at the change of topic. "I'm bringing dip." Good God, did she just say that? How lame.

The ballplayer tilted his head to the side and openly studied her. "What do you say to us going together? I'm taking a breather from dating. Clearing my head and all that, so I don't want to show up at this singles thing the night before Valentine's Day and be hassled by the ladies." He shot her a grin meant to coax her into agreement. "What do ya say?"

To spending an evening with him? Um, *yeah!* She'd be his beard anytime.

"I'll take that nod as a yes."

Bertie fought down the grasshoppers leaping in her belly and smiled shyly back. "It's a yes."

"Great. Pick you up at eight."

She could only stare, her mind reeling, as Drake slipped quietly into his apartment. Until something wet began soaking into her right mouse slipper, and Bertie looked down to see her dumping forgotten coffee all over the floor.

"Frick."

Chapter Two

DRAKE SHOVED A Rush ball cap over his tight curls and took a cursory glance at his plain leather wristwatch as it peeked out from under the cuff of his flannel shirt, noting the time. He'd dressed down for the party on purpose.

Hardly one for black tie on the best occasion, he quickly glanced down at his cream thermal Henley, faded jeans and red plaid flannel shirt with satisfaction. Looking like Paul Bunyan's homely cousin with a slightly smashed nose and baseball hat had its advantages. The ladies weren't generally into logger types.

"Don't want women getting the wrong impression," he grumbled as he shoved his wallet in his back pocket and grabbed his keys off the rack by the front door.

The past few months had soured him on the dating game and he was ready for a reprieve. Maybe it had something to do with seeing his teammates all hooking up and settling down this past year. Or maybe he was simply getting old. But the prospect of cozying up with some random cleat chaser for the night held about as much appeal as shampooing cat piss out of carpets.

Scratching the day's growth on his chin, Drake pondered briefly why that was and then pushed it aside. Maybe it was nothing more than a case of the same-old blues. His buddies all found women different from their norms. Just maybe that's what he needed too—a fresh perspective.

A short, curvy, bespectacled brunette came instantly to mind and he grinned. Now there was a fresh perspective if he'd ever seen one. The thought of spending the evening with her for company made the whole night seem more manageable. If he was lucky, she might spill vodka on her shirt and give him another strip tease.

He whistled under his breath as amusement filled him. That little mouse had a rack on her worthy of a center-stage spotlight on Broadway. Who'd have thought?

About to step through the doorway, Drake caught a glimpse of that morning's newspaper shoved haphazardly in his umbrella stand. He wondered what his favorite comic heroine had in store for her baseball love interest this week. He glanced at his watch and fought a quick internal tug-of-war. Part of him couldn't wait to read it, but the other part, that was borderline OCD when it came to punctuality, had noted that he was almost late for his non-date with his neighbor.

Heaving a big sigh, he stepped through the door and closed it quietly behind him. It was almost a compulsion—

this need to know the new installment of that damn comic. Whoever Roberta C was, she had a helluva wicked sense of humor and self-deprecating wit that had him in stitches every week. What had started out as appreciation for the comic-strip creator's mind had morphed into a secret crush for the real woman some two years ago. Right about the same time the heroine Bonnie had started stalking her ballplayer, actually.

Drake smirked and pocketed his keys. Heh. He wondered what it meant that those things happened at the same time. Probably coincidental, that's all. Wasn't it always?

Maybe he just needed a crazy little thing with big tits and bigger glasses—like Bonnie, in and out of the sack.

"Shit. Since when the hell am I so lonely?" He scoffed and strode the few steps to the door across the hall and knocked. He wasn't lonely. Guys like him didn't get lonely. They took breathers. Nice, long breathers.

Just like the one he was currently on.

Aw, damn it.

So maybe he was a little lonely. No big thing.

He was about to knock again when the door swung wide open. Instead, his hand froze in midair, a grin split his face, and his eyes lit up. Appreciation warmed his chest at the sight of Bertie in the doorway.

Now *this* was a woman after his own heart. His deep laughter echoed in the empty hallway.

"What?" She asked him, her eyes wide and seemingly innocent behind her glasses. "A woman can't protest society's oppressive and manufactured ideals on love and romance with a graphic T-shirt once in a while without getting hassled?"

Drake shook his head, still chuckling, and thought, *not when she has a picture of cartoon monkeys with hearts for eyes doing it smeared across her chest, along with the slogan* SCREW VALENTINE'S DAY, *she can't.*

Then he cleared his throat and said simply, "Nice shirt."

Bertie shook back her fluffy hair and smiled slightly. "It seemed appropriate given our situation."

He raised a brow, secretly impressed by the pair of balls she was sporting. He liked a woman who wasn't afraid to make a statement. "And what situation is that?"

The cutest rush of pink colored her cheeks and she glanced away, the large frame of her glasses slipping down her petite nose. "You know, our *non-date.*"

Her face instantly went from blushing pink to bright red, like saying the word out loud was too much. Drake took mercy on her, highly amused by the way she contradicted herself, at once both bold and shy. Tonight was ramping up to be much more enjoyable than he'd anticipated.

Tossing her a crooked grin, he offered her his elbow and said, "Well then, you wanna do this?"

She nodded once and reached for his arm. A slender hand slid around his elbow, heat trailing a path through his sleeve to him, taking him by surprise. Her fingers settled in the crook of his arm, the gentle movement feeling like a caress.

Well, he'd be damned. That was unexpected—one

tiny, unassuming brunette with pretty brown eyes was making his body come out of its stupor. What was he supposed to make of that?

Probably it was nothing more than a temporary glitch in his wiring. He liked Bertie just fine. She was unexpected and funny.

But she wasn't his type.

His conscience chose that moment to remind him that his *type* was boring him stupid. He had to give his conscience points. Touché.

Suddenly eager to get their non-date under way, Drake pulled his arm toward him, effectively tugging her up against his side. Grinning down at her wide-eyed expression, he joked, "Let's date, baby."

A snort escaped her, making Drake chuckle again. The sound was about as elegant as his aunt Martha after Thanksgiving dinner when she'd had one too many spiced ciders and started retelling her sordid years as a Hollywood makeup artist like they were the funniest stories in the world. But coming from Bertie it somehow managed to be cute instead of obnoxious.

"Date. *Right*." She muttered the words softly.

Drake didn't know whether to be offended or not. "Hey now, tiny thing." He squeezed her hand with the crook of his arm. "Play nice."

Her clear brown eyes went round. "Oh, no." She rushed. "That's not what I meant!" She stopped dead in her tracks, and he nearly yanked her forward before he realized it.

Taking in her expression, Drake frowned in concern. She'd gone three shades of white. "Whoa."

She yanked her hand out of his arm and blew out a frustrated breath. Then she threw her hands in the air and huffed, "Why does this always happen to me?" Considering he didn't know what *this* was, he figured he'd just keep his mouth shut.

"Why do words tumble out of my mouth like my brain just isn't connected?" She made a gesture with her hand, like a waterfall coming from her lips. "It's like I have verbal incontinence."

Surely he hadn't heard that right. Drake cocked his head and swallowed a smile. "What was that?"

She stomped her Vans and blew out a breath so hard it ruffled her bangs. "You know, like verbal diarrhea. I get so nervous that I say the wrong thing, and then I get so self-conscious that I said the wrong thing, I just talk and talk and talk and ramble on like an idiot," she finished, with a slump of her shoulders. "Awkward sucks."

His heart went out to her. "Aww, it can't be that bad."

Suddenly her gaze became intense and earnest. "Guess when the last time I had a date was? Like, an *actual* date."

He shrugged his shoulders. "Six months?" That seemed like a pretty decent dry spell to him.

Bertie snorted again and shoved her hands in the front pockets of her jeans. "*Pssh*. I wish."

Getting into the spirit of the conversation, Drake took a good look at his neighbor—from her fluffy brown hair to her scuffed shoes. Under the suggestive shirt and loose-fitted jeans was a curvy, womanly body. She had good skin. It was clear and flushed with health and vitality. And her hair looked soft.

The wrapping wasn't flashy, but the product was real nice and solid. His body stirred as he looked her over.

He took a guess. "A year." It couldn't be more than that. Bertie was charming, in an offbeat sort of way.

She rolled her eyes, making him laugh and they started walking again. "Try over two years."

Disbelief filled him. "Get out." What was wrong with guys these days?

"No, it's true." She started as she caught up to him. "Last one was a blind date from TrueMatch.com. And even though the guy brought his *mother*, he decided *I* wasn't his type. He said, and I quote, 'You could put some effort into it, you know.'"

Drake wanted to punch the mama's boy in his wimpy face. "Screw that. You look plenty good."

Clear brown eyes with golden flecks glanced up curiously at him. "You think so?"

He nodded, feeling oddly protective. "You want me to beat him up for you?" He was only half joking.

Her slender shoulders relaxed and she laughed quietly. "Nah, I handled it. I excused myself to the bathroom, then went to the bar and ordered four bottles of their most expensive wine. And then I left out the back, sticking him and his mommy with the bill."

He threw back his head and laughed with appreciation. "Feisty!"

They reached the elevator at the far end of the hall and he hit the UP button.

Feeling eager all of a sudden, he couldn't help but

glance down at his companion with the crude T-shirt and black librarian glasses. Something stirred deep in the pit of his stomach, something totally abstract and foreign. He wouldn't exactly call it uncomfortable, but it was completely new, so he was kind of leery of the unsettling feeling.

Leery—but not outright opposed.

Huh. *Weird.*

The *ding* of the elevator startled him, and he jerked his gaze away. Clearing his throat he asked with forced casualness, "So why's a girl like you got a problem landing a cuddle partner?"

She looked at him like he was stupid—plain stupid and she just couldn't comprehend the enormity of it. "Uhh, because I'm a *nerd*." She gestured down her body in a fast, frustrated movement. "Do you *see* me?"

Drake let his eyes wander real slow down her body. *All* the way down—and then *all* the way back up. It wasn't bad. Not bad at all. But it was the sass under the frump that he was really starting to dig. Made him wonder briefly what else she was hiding.

"Yep. I see you all right."

"If you see me, then you shouldn't even have to ask such an obvious question to begin with."

Smart women were a complicated lot. That's the reason why he'd made himself comfortable for a good long time with brainless, empty things. The last time he'd tangoed with a woman with both brains and attitude, he'd married her and then found himself divorced five years later, when she'd run off with his tax accountant—taking half his assets and all of his heart.

He'd wanted a huge brood with her—a loud, crazy but happy family with her. Shit, he loved kids. They were truth and life personified—so whole and pure and untainted. And accepting. God, they were accepting. He needed that in his life. Just plain needed to be accepted and loved for who he was.

And Drake had thought he'd had that with Pam. Turned out he couldn't have been more wrong. When she'd told him she was pregnant he'd thought something was off with the timing, but he'd been so damn thrilled at the prospect of being a dad that he'd shrugged the feelings aside. Then the excitement had settled a little, just enough for him to really start to think about where he had been during the time of conception. And the hell of it was, he was pretty sure he'd still been down in Florida for spring training. His questioning her about it had brought out the truth of her affair.

Dating shallow and less than intelligent women had allowed him to hide the pain. They'd never cared to see beyond his wallet or his fame to the man he really was. And he'd been more than okay with that.

It was only recently that his feelings had changed.

Drake stepped into the open elevator and held the door for her, giving her a raised-eyebrow look. "Seems to me like somebody's got a self-confidence issue going on."

She huffed and her bangs fluffed again as she stepped in beside him. Her head didn't even reach his shoulder. "Do not," she muttered but avoided his gaze.

The sheer stubbornness he heard in her tone made his lips twitch. "Might be wrong, but just sayin'. Maybe if you worked on that, you'd stop having man-finding troubles and land yourself a real fine keeper."

He couldn't be sure, but she mumbled something under her breath that sounded an awful lot like, "Maybe if you stopped dating bimbos, you'd see what was right in front of you."

A ball of heat flared in his chest, catching him off guard.

Well, if that didn't just beat all. His world was simply full of surprises today.

Drake leaned down to prod her about it, intent on finding out if that's what she'd really said. He'd just caught a whiff of her hair and was momentarily distracted by the fresh scent when she jerked straight as a lance and shouted, "*Dip!* I forgot the dip!"

Next thing he knew she was leaping from the elevator and running down the hall as fast as her beat-out Vans would take her, effectively squashing his chance to question her. Disappointment hit him. Until he saw her skid to a halt in front of her door, holding up a finger to him as she rifled for her keys—doing it all in a tizzy as she hollered back to him, "Don't go! I'll be right back!"

Now he wasn't disappointed. Oh no. Not by a long shot.

Now he was just flat-out amused.

She returned, flushed and a little out of breath a few minutes later, cradling a ceramic bowl to her chest like she was bear-hugging it. "Thanks for waiting."

His chest warmed at the words, like she was talking about a different kind of waiting altogether. "Anytime."

They rode the elevator up, talking everything from baseball to politics to that comic strip they both liked. Bertie's sharp sense of humor had him laughing even as they argued the logic behind Bonnie's belief that she was cursed to live the anti-charmed life.

"She's just an average woman with an average life, Drake. No matter how hard she tries, or what she does, she'll never rise above mediocrity. She's shy, not particularly courageous or graceful, and nobody ever seems to notice her. That's why she's an archivist for the Natural History museum. Her brief touch with greatness through her obsession with the ballplayer is her one big silver lining in all the drab dullness that is her life."

"You got it all wrong, sweet thing. She's not average—not by a long shot. Bonnie's the woman everyone underestimates because she's not flashy, but she's anything but mediocre. Maybe a few screws loose, but so what? She's hella courageous. Remember that time she broke into the ballplayer's place when he was on an away trip and sniffed all his underwear, even snagging a few?" It made him laugh just thinking about it.

She nodded. "Yeah, but—"

Drake shook his head, feeling mighty defensive of his sweet little Bonnie. "No buts, girlie. It took balls for her to do it. Finesse, too. Plus, the way she finds such personal gifts shows thoughtfulness on her part. She pays attention. And if that dipshit player would get his head out of his ass he'd see that she's the perfect woman for him." He thought he was finished, but felt some emotion well up in him and he blurted out, "She's got heart, damn it. A guy needs a little heart now and then."

Feeling a little embarrassed by his outburst, Drake crossed his arms and shrugged his shoulders when Bertie looked up at him with huge, round questioning eyes. "What?" He asked gruffly. "The road can be a cold, lonely place after a while for a ballplayer. Having something warm and sweet like Bonnie to come home to wouldn't be so bad. That guy needs to wise up. Just sayin'." Drake tried for a frown, but couldn't pull it off. God he was soft.

"You surprise me." Those brown eyes looked up at him and seemed to sparkle with an inner light.

He got lost in the beauty of them and felt something inside him start to shift. "How's that?"

She smiled gently, just the slightest curve of her full lips, and whatever had started to shift simply changed into something else entirely. Though he couldn't place it, Drake knew it had to do with the petite brunette currently staring up at him.

"You're more than you seem. More than just "Crazy Drake" the ballplayer." The way she said it made it sound like a compliment.

He decided he liked being complimented by Bertie. "And so is Bonnie."

She rolled her eyes and grinned. "Are we back to that?"

He could feel himself getting worked up all over again and smiled. Debating with his little smart-mouthed neighbor was quickly becoming one of his favorite activities. "Girl, we never left. We'll stay here all day until you see things my way."

She scoffed at his bluster, clearly unimpressed, making him laugh, and he realized that what had changed for him was his interest in Bertie. It had gone from mild to something far more significant.

It had suddenly become very, very personal.

Chapter Three

BERTIE WAS STILL deeply into their debate when the elevator door opened at their destination—and all the thoughts in her head promptly exploded into a million little pieces. A big *What the hell?* immediately replaced them.

The tenth floor hallway stretched out in front of them— one long, pink-and-red horror of a decorated corridor that vaguely resembled a woman's vagina in an oddly uncomfortable and awkward way.

Especially considering that Geoff, the man who'd decorated this monstrosity was as gay as Lady Gaga was fabulous. Bertie didn't know what to make of it. But she must have been the only one, by the look of singles milling about with spiked punch, laughing and appearing happy in their various I'm-available-and-aren't-I-awesome-you-know-you-want-me outfits.

She rolled her eyes. It *was* a singles party. They were probably just drunk—nerves making them take a few more sips than necessary. Besides, that punch was Geoff's specialty drink. Bertie suspected he put more than a generous helping of vodka into the mix. On more than one occasion she'd table-danced after a glass or three of his brew.

And Bertie Cogswell table dancing was not a pretty sight. Oh no, it was not. It was a recipe for pure mortification the morning after for everyone who witnessed the event. And considering that she'd had enough humiliation for a lifetime already, Bertie decided to steer clear of the punch.

A huge hand settled at the base of her spine, the heat and hardness of which sunk into her skin, making it tingle. There was a part of her brain that couldn't believe Drake Paulson had just placed his hand on her lower back, the part that made her eyes want to go all cartoon huge.

It feels so good.

Just as the thought registered and shock snapped her body straight, that rather hard, hot hand slipped ever so casually lower until it was resting on her left butt cheek.

Her eyebrows shot into her bangs and her eyes nearly popped from her head. Air rushed from her lungs on a garbled, "Whoa!"

Before her brain could grasp what was happening, the scent of wood, spice and man filled her nose in a heady, intoxicating mix and a very hard, very masculine body was leaning down over her, the heat coming off his massive frame a full-scale sensual assault.

She almost dropped the dip.

Bertie had never experienced anything like having Drake Paulson curled around her, touching her. Her heart beat a frantic, nervous rhythm, and her brain had gone blank like someone hitting the DELETE button.

A deep, thoroughly male chuckle rumbled his chest. The sound of it so rugged and manly, heat flared instantly to life between her legs. *Get a grip, Bertie!*

It was Drake Paulson. He dated everyone but her. This had to be a joke.

Suddenly his breath was fanning softly over her ear, and whether it was a joke or not, her body didn't care. She went wet.

"This is very interesting," came his warm, gravelly voice from next to her ear. And having it live in her ear was so much better than any fantasy she'd ever had. It was rich and smoky and made her think of wood fires and cashmere blankets.

Swallowing hard, Bertie grabbed for control—and failed miserably. "You're touching my butt!" she squeaked, totally out of sorts. And then she wanted to slap herself for stating the obvious like an idiot.

Laughter rumbled in his chest again and the hand currently resting on her behind curled, squeezing her cheek gently. "Glad you noticed. And yeah, call it a test."

Bertie opened her mouth to ask him what he meant just as a figure approached and demanded, "Just what do you two think you're doing in here?"

Completely disoriented and feeling a pang of disappointment as Drake pulled away, Bertie blinked and forced her eyes to focus on the body standing out in the hallway. When she saw who it was, her confusion cleared and she was swamped with irritation.

It was a Hollywood Barbie wannabe, all decked out in a skanky red-lace bodysuit and platform heels. Her perfectly bleached hair swung over her shoulder as she tossed her head and pasted on a big fake smile for the ballplayer standing next to Bertie. She'd seen her type a thousand times.

Drake's type.

"Well, hello there, handsome! I was beginning to wonder if you'd show. You never answered my text, you silly man," the tramp said as she latched on to his arm and tried to pull him from the elevator.

Bertie glanced up to see his reaction and instantly regretted it. His firm lips were curled in a smile and those basset-hound brown eyes of his practically sparkled, they twinkled so bright. And it had to be because of the bimbo now clamped on to his arm.

I mean, who else? she thought as her stomach sank.

It certainly couldn't be because of her.

"Excuse me," Bertie said, suddenly desperate to be out of the elevator and away from Drake Paulson and his bimbo. Pushing her way clear, she didn't stop even when she heard him shout, "Where are you going?"

Waving dismissively over her shoulder, she called out breezily, "The party needs my dip, Drake. Catch you later!"

The words might have sounded casual but her insides were shaking. How could she entertain, even for the briefest break from sanity, any possible universe in which Drake Paulson would be interested in her, Bertie-freakin'-Cogswell? Whatever had happened in the elevator was clearly a mistake—an accident.

Before this morning, he hadn't even known she existed.

That thought sobered her as she pushed her way through the throng of eager singles and made her way into the host's super-posh condo. The minute she crossed the threshold, dip in hand, a shadow fell across her vision. It was accompanied by the very distinct scent of mint Lifesavers and pepperoni Hot Pockets, the smell almost making her gag.

Oh God. *Bobby Murkus.*

"Well, if it isn't Bertie Cogswell! Still sassy and single as ever, I see. I was hoping I'd run into you here!"

Yeah, she just bet. Bobby was the building's biggest nerd and he had a very obvious crush on her. For the past two months she'd been avoiding going to the sixth floor at any expense, even though poor arthritic Mrs. Daxter—who looked forward to their weekly gossip sessions while Bertie set and curled her hair for her—lived right next door to him. But since Mrs. Daxter didn't get out much and they both enjoyed the time, Bertie had begged the teenage boy down the hall with the faux-hawk and black eyeliner to escort the lady to Bertie's place every Thursday.

That hadn't worked, but money had.

Desperate times called for desperate measures. And after what had happened the last time the smelly computer geek had caught her all alone, there was simply no way in hell she was going to risk a repeat. It was so worth paying the kid.

Like a cold, slimy snake had just slithered down her back, Bertie shivered when Bobby leaned in close to her ear. The ear that Drake had almost caressed mere minutes ago in a *much* better way. The offensive mixture of smells made her nose hairs curl as he said with his wheezy, whiny voice, "Have you given any more thought to my proposal"

Though her brain tried to block it, the memory surfaced before it could be stopped and Bertie was thrown back to the last time they were together. The side-part-sporting, suspender-wearing Class-A nerd had kissed her full on the lips and proposed to her. His reasoning—he swore up and down about all of its logic and sense and their matching algorithms (whatever *that* meant—was that people like them didn't get the cream of the crop. They had to settle. And he wanted Bertie to be his "settle partner."

The thought of settling at all, and that he even *saw* her as somebody in that category—the one where everyone in it had to accept far less than what they wanted—was so monumentally depressing that she'd told him to suck it in rather loud, impolite terms and run off crying.

And to have him here, right now, after her brief heavenly encounter with the man of her dreams, reminded her of everything that she *wasn't* and could never have. It made her want to lash out in denial and punch him in his dorky, chubby face.

Bertie didn't want to settle. Oh no. Her eye was on someone clear at the top.

She wanted Drake.

All she needed was the courage to go and get him. He'd said she needed self-esteem. Well, now was a really good time to find some before he ended up heading back to his apartment with a woman who was totally wrong for him.

God, could she really do it? Did she really have the *cajones*?

Bertie glanced over at Bobby—her *future* (shiver) if she chose to accept it—and made a decision. She'd never know what she might have if she never went for it. Why settle when she'd never even tried shooting for the stars to begin with?

Jazzed at this newfound resolve and confidence, Bertie pushed Bobby away. "God, Bobby. Give a girl some personal space, will you?" Her palm landed on him and all she could think was how hard Drake's body was compared to his squishy one—and how much she *liked* it.

Yeah, settling wasn't an option. "And before you ask me again, the answer is no. No now—and no forever. It will never, *ever* happen." She tried to brush past him. "If you'll excuse me, I have dip to deliver."

She did her best snooty hair fling and threw her shoulders back. Speaking her mind felt *good*.

"You'll reconsider, just you watch!" Bobby called out behind her, his voice confident and sure. "We're meant for each other!"

Eww. Really, universe, really? She deserved better than that. Didn't she?

"There you are! *Thank, God.* This party has been utterly dismal without you!" Geoff latched his slender hand on her arm in a vice grip, his manicured fingernails digging in sharply.

"Ouch!"

Instantly apologetic, he loosened his grip and shot her big forgive-me eyes. "So sorry, love. It's just—*ugh!*" Her friend stomped his foot in a dramatic display and rolled his eyes, his inner queen in full effect. It's one of the things she adored about him. Geoff was even bitchier than she was.

He leaned in to her and whispered fiercely, "Do you know who had the fucking *balls* to show his face at my party?" He didn't even wait for her to answer. "That's right, honey. D'angelo. After what that bastard did to me?"

Bertie gave him a sympathetic look and handed him her bowl of dip. "Here, take this. I feel like I've been holding it forever. And I know. It's tough."

Geoff pressed his cheek to hers briefly and straightened. She couldn't help admiring the way his chestnut hair shimmered under the lights. He was such a gorgeous specimen of man. And D'angelo, the wannabe Broadway star, was so far beneath him.

Suddenly filled with conviction, Bertie put her hands on Geoff's impressive biceps, stared into his light green eyes, and declared, "Whatever you do, don't settle! That loser doesn't deserve you. He stole your pillowcases, for crissake!"

He instantly frowned. "Those were custom-made, two-thousand-thread-count organic Egyptian cotton, too, the prick."

Catching sight of Drake entering the apartment, his

Rush ball cap and massive shoulders towering over most of the people in attendance, Bertie nodded as her stomach went six kinds of jittery. "Umm-hmm," she replied to her friend even though she was no longer paying him any attention. How could she when her dream guy was standing across the room and she was almost pumped up enough to go for it and tell him how she felt?

Out of the corner of her eye she saw Bobby wave at her and grin his smug, dorky grin—like he knew the inevitable outcome and was just watching, waiting for her to come around to the same conclusion.

Never.

She turned to Geoff. "Don't you dare even talk to that man, you understand? He's bad news." It was her duty as his friend to tell him the truth.

"You think I can get that great big hunk of beefcake over there to kick him out for me?" Her friend nodded toward Drake. And she had to agree. He was a great big hunk of beefcake.

"Oh my God, *fabulous*. He's coming this way!" Geoff ended with an excited squeeze on her arm as Drake made his way toward them. He snagged a couple glasses of champagne from a nearby table and continued, a smile on his lips that made her stomach flip excitedly.

Geoff elbowed her in the side. "Hands off, sweetie. He's mine."

She couldn't blame her bestie for trying to stake a claim. "You know he's straight, right?"

Green eyes full of naughty looked at her. "Not after one night with me, he's not."

Knowing he was joking, she laughed and kissed his cheek. "Dream on, darling."

Drake came to a stop a few feet from them and Bertie had to crane her neck back to look into his eyes. She decided to take the scenic route and admired his broad shoulders on the way up. The way they filled out his flannel shirt was just *so nice*.

By the time her gaze had meandered up to meet his, her cheeks felt flushed—and it wasn't with embarrassment. The man was put together in the best possible way. Whew.

Geoff spoke up. "Drake Paulson, so fabulous to see you!" The way he smiled at the ballplayer made her want to kick him in the shins. *She* had dibs.

"Yeah, thanks for the invite. Nice party." Drake said with a look around. "From what I hear, it's all because of Bertie's dip." His lips twitched after he finished saying that and he winked down at her.

Geoff just stared at him in confusion. "I'm not sure I understand."

Of course he didn't, it was an inside joke. Taking pity on him, Bertie nudged him gently toward the kitchen. "Why don't you go put that bowl down so everybody can have some?"

Their host suddenly laughed. "Oh, you mean *this* dip!"

Bertie shot him a look. "Yeah, what else?"

Her friend just shook his head and replied, "It *is* fabulous. I'll be right back. Miss me." He shot over his shoulder with a grin as he melted into the party crowd.

As soon as he was gone, Drake handed her a glass, a

look of pure mischief on his face. "How about we make tonight interesting, tiny thing?"

Like it wasn't already? Elevator, *hello*. But she played it cool and accepted the champagne. "Yeah, how so?"

He grinned like the devil. "Every time Geoff says the word "fabulous" we have to take a drink."

God, it was the man's favorite word. "We'll be drunk before he even breaks out his karaoke machine."

The rascal just raised a brow. "And?"

And nothing. "You're on."

"Fabulous."

They were still laughing when Geoff rejoined them. "What're we laughing about?"

Bertie shook her head and swallowed around the giggle in her throat. "Nothing, really." Then she tried to divert his attention. "Look at how many people showed up, you awesome host." Her hand gestured loosely at the crowd.

He beamed at her and Drake. "I know! Isn't it fabulous? Somebody's even setting up beer pong in the dining room. How retro is that?"

Drake's eye caught hers and they both grinned before taking drinks of their champagne at the same time. "It is that." She finally managed to say.

Within five minutes, Geoff had said the word so many times their glasses were empty, and Bertie was starting to feel loose limbed and a little giddy. Champagne always went straight to her head. She was just about to say so when Drake grabbed her hand in one of his and declared, "To beer pong!"

Bertie could only wave over her shoulder at Geoff as the ballplayer tugged her along behind him. Not that she was complaining. Oh no. Thanks to her bestie and his overused adjective she was feeling just fine.

There was quite a group of people gathered in the dining room when they arrived and she could see the games were just about to start. The beer cups were set up on each end, but where were the teams?

Apparently Drake was wondering the same thing, because he hollered to the room at large, "Who's playing, people? Me and the lady want in."

"You got it, Paulson!" Someone said.

The next thing she knew, she and Drake were side by side and she was tossing a Ping-Pong ball at a pyramid of plastic beer cups. For the next ten minutes she chugged beer and bounced plastic balls across a table with the man of her dreams at her side. And it turned out that she had a knack for beer pong, the other team's empty cups and slightly green expressions proof.

Riding high on the win, Drake picked her up in a bear hug and spun her around. "Way to go, little mouse!"

He set her back down gently, but before she could take it all in, the crowd moved in on them. Or more specifically, on Drake. She was soundly pushed to the side by all the people who suddenly couldn't wait to get their hands on the famous ballplayer.

"Hey, Paulson. How 'bout we partner this time?" Called some guy with a red Polo shirt, wingtips and a thirty-dollar haircut.

"Wait, I want a turn with Paulson!" A woman from the back shouted out.

"No, he's *mine*!" Another woman hollered back.

Still another female voice joined the mix and pretty soon there was a whole lot of arguing and shoving, the chance of being his beer-pong partner suddenly the prize of a lifetime and worth fighting for. Next thing she knew, she'd been jostled all the way out of the room and Drake had been swallowed by the crowd.

Disappointed, but trying to take it in stride, Bertie made her way back through the apartment to the kitchen. Once there she spotted her dip laid out on the counter with other appetizers and scooped up some with a tortilla chip. She took a bite and sighed. Man, it really was *fabulous*.

She decided to hide out in the kitchen for a while, chatting occasionally with those she knew. When she'd filled up on food, she went in search of Geoff. She found him in the living room. Stepping up next to him, Bertie was about to speak when she spotted Drake across the room.

And, she couldn't help but notice, that he was suddenly quite squarely in the middle of a swarm of gold diggers in various slutty getups and looking not at all unhappy about it. In fact, if his amused expression was any indication of how he was feeling, she'd bet that he was pretty damn happy about it.

Her heart sank as she stared at him surrounded by the type of woman she would never be—beautiful, thin women that every man wanted. And when he raised a thick, well-shaped eyebrow at her and shot her a grin that was all hot, sexed-up male, she felt her newfound confidence dissolve into nothingness.

Drake Paulson could only be smiling that way for one reason. Well, more like ten reasons. And they were standing all around him. It certainly wasn't because of the awesome game of beer pong they'd shared.

Yes, he'd invited her to the party. Yes, he'd been polite and even spent time with her once they were there. He'd even seemed to enjoy her company.

But he hadn't smiled like that.

In an instant it all became clear: Drake was out of her league. Would always *be* out of her league. And that meant that Bobby might be right after all. Maybe she should just give up and stop dreaming.

Maybe she *should* settle.

Oh God!

Emotions wracked Bertie, one on top of another, and sent her world spinning. Denial slammed into her chest and flared there, searing hot. It couldn't be!

She needed to get out of there now.

Leaving Geoff with a barely intelligible good-bye, Bertie shoved her way through the crowd. Her eyes were locked on the exit. She refused to look anywhere else. As she passed a table with various wine bottles on it, she reached a hand out blindly and grabbed one.

If she had to settle, it sure as hell wasn't going to be there.

Chapter Four

DRAKE WATCHED WITH a sinking feeling in his gut as Bertie swiped a bottle of champagne and left. She had *not* looked happy and he was pretty sure he knew why. He'd had an urge and tested the waters with her in the elevator. He'd shown his interest and everything had been going well. Then there'd been the beer-pong mob. Their time together had been nixed. He'd been trying to make his way back to her all night with no success. By the way she'd scowled at him and stomped off just now, after he'd given her his sexy smile in apology, he was pretty sure she wasn't up for getting to know him in an intimate way.

It was a real drag.

This whole day had turned upside down and he wasn't sure what to make of things. First he'd been on a breather, then his little quirky neighbor with the great body had grabbed his attention—much to his surprise. And just when he'd been spending time with her and enjoying it immensely, the flash mob had thrown a bucket of cold water on everything.

Part of him couldn't believe how upset he was at Bertie leaving. It was the same part that had been feeling the emptiness in his life lately. And it wanted to track her down and find out *exactly* what was what. He thought about it for a minute and had a realization. That "part" was *all* of him.

Drake surveyed the scene before him. Almost a dozen cleat chasers vied for his attention, every last one of them hoping to score with the rich professional ballplayer. Six months ago that wouldn't have bothered him. Hell, he'd have been all over it. No commitment, no danger of heartache.

But then, as his teammates had paired off one after the other in rapid succession, he'd been left with a whole lot of Friday nights all to himself. He'd had to *be* with himself. It wasn't very long before he couldn't ignore himself anymore. And that's when he'd started to have some honest conversations with himself.

Now, standing face-to-face with a room full of what he didn't want—not anymore—after what his gut was beginning to tell him he *did* want had just left in a huff, made it impossible to deny.

He wanted to find his other half too.

His mind was suddenly quite made up. "Step to the side, girlies. I'm making my way through. I've got somewhere to be."

Ignoring the protests, Drake moved quickly through

the crowd and headed to the elevator. If he was guessing right, Bertie had just gone home. He'd stop there first, see if she was in.

Then what was he going to do?

That wasn't entirely clear to him at the moment, but he'd figure it out.

As it turned out, he didn't have to figure out anything. When he stepped out of the elevator on their floor, Bertie was sitting on the carpet with her back to her door. The bottle of Cristal she'd swiped from the party dangled loosely from her fingers.

Her head whipped in his direction when the elevator doors closed behind him and she wobbled a bit. "Hey there, Drakey Drake." She slurred the words as she gave him an overly bright smile.

Amusement sparked in his chest. Looked like the little mouse was drunk. "What're you doing sitting out here all by yourself, tiny thing?"

Her hand waved lazily at her door. "Locked out. Musta left the keys inside when I went back for the dip. Damn dip." She ended on a grumble and glared at the door.

Already lowering himself, Drake asked, "Mind if I join you?" No way was he going to pass up the opportunity of seeing Bertie loosened up and unfiltered, on champagne. For as much as she must run her mouth on a normal day, he bet it didn't even compare after a few glasses of bubbly. And he couldn't wait to hear everything she had to say.

He'd already sat down by the time she squinted at him and scrunched her nose up like she smelled something foul. "Already bored of all those long, skinny model legs that go from here," she pointed at the floor by her feet, "to clear over there?" she ended by gesturing to the end of the hall.

More than he'd realized. "Actually, yeah."

His admission must not have been what she expected to hear because she started to say something and then just kind of sputtered to a stop with her eyes big and round. "Wha—? Wait. Really?"

Shifting his shoulders, he settled in more comfortably and chuckled, still surprised by the truth of it himself. "Yeah, really."

She eyed him for a second and then said with a haughty little sniff, "Then you can sit down."

He didn't have the heart to point out that he already was.

Instead he reached for the bottle of Cristal and their fingers brushed briefly, just long enough for a single jolt of electricity to shoot up his arm at the connection. Bertie jerked her hand away, and he brought the bottle to his lips, took a sip. The fizzy drink made his nose tingle.

When he was done he said, "Want me to find Ruben for you and have him let you in with his master key?"

Bertie was already shaking her head before he'd finished his question. "Can't." She hiccupped softly and continued, "He and the Boobs are gettin' it on. Saw 'em in one of Geoff's bedrooms when I was leaving."

Everybody in the building knew that the superintendent didn't answer his phone when he was knocking boots with "the Boobs"—the filthy-rich divorcée so named because of the fake tits she'd bought herself as a "morale booster" during her separation. They were half the size of Texas. Literally. They entered the room way before she did.

Drake looked down at his companion, felt his blood start to stir, and gave the Boobs a mental high-five for waylaying the super for a while. He liked the idea of getting to just sit and talk with Bertie. He liked the idea a whole lot. "Looks like it's just you and me then."

"You'll miss the party."

"Never really wanted to go to it anyway, remember? Ain't no big thing." Drake grabbed the bottle and took another drink. "Besides, I think we should talk about what happened in the elevator before you bolted."

She didn't agree. "Oh no. You mean before that, that *woman* barged in and interrupted. What was with her *outfit*?"

Was that sharp edge in her tone jealousy? "I don't know what you mean . . ."

Like she was morally affronted, Bertie's mouth dropped wide open and she shot him a look. One of *those* looks. "Oh, come on. Are you that used to the show, *Mr. Baseball*, that you don't even notice anymore?"

Drake's brows shot up. "What's that supposed to mean?" He was pretty sure he should be offended.

Her hands flew into motion. "I've seen your women! They all look the same, all dressed up in nothing, parading about. Just to get your attention."

"Hey now, it hasn't been all that bad." Or had it? Judging by the look of distaste on her face it would probably be fair to say that yes, it had been. In his defense, he'd had good reason for swimming in the shallow end of the pool. But maybe he'd gone a little overboard with the whole easy, no-depth-no-commitment thing.

Listening to Bertie, you'd think that he was just as bad as the ballplayer in his favorite comic—the unrepentant lady's man. And that thought led to another. "You sound like Bonnie from that comic. Are you spying on me too?"

He'd meant it as a joke, but her face went pale and suddenly she snatched up the champagne, taking a good long glug. After wiping the back of her hand across her lips, she replied, "Whatever. Your love life doesn't impress me."

"So you've been paying attention to my love life, then?" That was interesting. Why would Bertie care? Before this morning they hadn't said more than a few polite words to each other. Which, now that he thought about it, was really too bad. It felt a bit like two good years had been wasted.

He thought of the cleat chasers at the party upstairs and couldn't help but wonder if he would have been in a place to really appreciate what Bertie had to offer. Honest truth was, probably not.

Everything happens in its own time, he thought, just as a couple stepped out of the elevator to his left, both of them speaking very loudly.

"Geoff always throws *the best* parties!" The brunette in the poufy skirt exclaimed. "I don't know why on earth he can't find someone. It's sad really. I've been to the last three of his parties and it's the same sob story with him."

Her male companion, in faded-black skinny jeans,

replied pointedly, "But you've gone three years in a row too."

She stopped and demanded, "What does that mean? Are you implying that I'm a sob story too?"

The poor guy was clearly oblivious to the hornet's nest he'd just opened. Drake cringed because he could see the fight brewing.

The woman's companion just shrugged and said, "You know . . ."

The brunette slapped her hands on her hips and screeched, "No, *I don't know*, Scott. Are you calling me a shrew now? Saying I'm unlovable?"

Poor guy had his foot in it now. "No, I—"

She shoved him aside and flew past Drake and Bertie, knocking the champagne bottle over onto Bertie as they passed.

"Hey, watch it!" she cried out.

But it was too late. She'd been just about to take a drink, but instead Cristal had splashed all over the front of her graphic T-shirt and soaked it, the thin pink fabric becoming almost translucent. From his viewpoint, Drake could clearly see the outline of her bra and the swell of her breasts through the wet, clingy fabric.

Lust stirred in the pit of his stomach at the sight of her full, gorgeously round breasts so temptingly displayed. He couldn't help but wonder what they would look like completely bare and exposed to him. And here he'd been starting to think that a repeat of her ripping off her shirt wasn't going to happen.

Because he couldn't resist, Drake raised a hand and

waggled his fingers at her chest. "Your *you knows* are showing again."

Bertie gasped and slapped a hand over the wet spot, effectively blocking his view. "Damn it!" She searched left and right quickly, like she was looking for something to mop it up with, but came away empty and demanded instead, "What are you doing looking at them?"

Because he was a guy. And because she had great tits. There'd be something wrong with him if he *didn't* look. "You need some help?" The glare she shot him had him chuckling and dying to push her buttons some more. "I could lick it off for you."

This time her gasp was strong enough to rock her back against the door. "You would not!"

Drake leaned down and whispered in her ear, taking in the faint herbal scent of her shampoo. "Wanna bet?"

The speed at which her face went from white to beet red made him laugh outright, even as arousal made his body hum in anticipation. Her fresh and honest response to his flirting was such a welcome reprieve from the practiced ones he was used to receiving. Everything about Bertie was refreshing.

And Drake suddenly realized what he'd been missing out on by hiding out from real relationships these past few years. His teammate JP Trudeau kept telling him it was time to find something real and stop wasting his time with cheap women. Apparently the kid was right.

Because now that he had discovered the wonderful world that was Bertie he wasn't in any hurry to let it go.

Running on instinct, Drake gently kissed the top of

her ear, letting the tip of his tongue just barely touch her skin.

She shivered and sucked in a breath. "What are you doing?" She asked in a voice gone breathy and a little strained.

Lost in the feel of her, Drake softly trailed a fingertip down the side of her neck, "Seeing what's going on here."

Bertie jolted and dropped the bottle again. More liquid splashed on her thigh and soaked her jeans. Her head swung toward him, her glasses bumping him in the nose and dislodging. They fell onto her lap and then across the floor. One lens popped out of the frame and fell out onto the carpet.

Letting out a huge sigh, she closed her eyes and leaned her head back against the door. "Man, just . . . just . . . fuck my life."

The way she said it had him sitting upright, a buzz starting in his head. Like he'd been struck by a lightning bolt, Drake stared hard at Bertie, something jogging his mind. She sounded just like Bonnie from that comic strip!

Wait a second. Drake narrowed his eyes on her, suddenly seeing her in a whole different light. From her fluffy brown hair and chunky black glasses to her smart mouth and witty sense of humor . . . how had he missed it? Bertie was *exactly* like the comic heroine! No, she was more than that. She *was* Bonnie.

More precisely, he suspected she was Roberta C, the hilarious and sarcastic comic-strip creator. The very same woman he'd fantasized and wondered about. The one whose mind and words had him so entranced that he couldn't miss a single installment of her series without feeling seriously down about it, like he'd missed something vital and important. Hell, he even carried a stapled-together collection of her weekly comics in his bag for away games so he'd have something of hers to read while he was on the road.

It blew his freaking mind.

And it made his heart pound furiously in his chest, so hard and fast it almost hurt. How could it be? What was the probability of his crush living *right next door* this whole time? "It's you, isn't it?" he finally asked, his voice filled with awe. "You're *her*."

Bertie's eyes darted away and she tried to scramble to her feet, but he stopped her with a hand. "I don't know what you mean. You're just talking crazy." She did jazz hands and smiled wobbly. "*Crazy* Drake."

No he wasn't. The truth of his realization rocked him. He knew he was right.

He'd just been too big a fool to see it.

But he saw it now and wasn't going to waste any more time. Reaching out with his other hand, which shook slightly, he cupped her soft, rounded cheek gently and said with his heart in his throat, "Kiss me."

He didn't wait for her answer.

Chapter Five

BERTIE HAD NO time to prepare before Drake's lips came down on hers. At the connection, her brain melted like butter in the sun. It was like it simply couldn't comprehend the fact that the man of her dreams was kissing her and had just ceased to exit.

It felt *amazing*.

Like everything she'd ever imagined, cranked up about a thousand degrees. The man had lips that should have been as hard as the rest of him. Instead they were soft and sensual and oh, so warm. They moved against hers in gentle exploration, the unexpected sensuality of it making her moan helplessly. And when his body leaned in to hers and she was surrounded by all the virile ruggedness that was Drake Paulson, she forgot herself completely and groaned against his lips, "Oh God, yes."

It was like she'd been waiting for this moment her

whole life. For the moment when his lips touched hers. And it was here and it was now and she'd had just enough champagne to not give a damn. She was meant for this.

Throwing her arms around his neck, she dove head-long into the kiss.

"Bertie, are you here? Bertie, *where are you*?"

Like she'd been dunked in an ice tank, she froze. Oh God, no. Not him! Not *now*.

Drake pulled back, a frown tugging at his brows. "What the hell?"

"It's Bobby Murkus." She whispered raggedly as something close to panic gripped her. The last thing she wanted was for him to say something to Drake that would ruin this for her. "Quick. Let's go to your place."

She was already on her feet and grabbing at his flannel sleeve before he'd even stood up, openly frowning now. "He causing you trouble?"

"Oh, there you are! I've been looking all over for you!" She could see Bobby down the hall behind Drake. He was quickly making his way toward her and eyeing the ballplayer cautiously. "What are you doing with him? I thought we had an unspoken agreement."

Bertie opened her mouth to speak to tell him only in his deluded head, but Drake grabbed her around the waist and pulled her into his side—his very muscular, very hard side. *Oh my*. Then he began walking them both to his apartment door. And suddenly she didn't mind so much that the most annoying man on the planet was walking toward her. Not when she had Drake's incredible body pressed up against hers.

It was a dream—well, more like a *million* dreams—come true.

"Sorry, pal. The lady's taken," her fantasy man stated very firmly over her shoulder. The way he said it, so gruff and possessive, made her heart leap for joy. But before she could think on its significance, he whisked her through the door to his place, slamming the door shut in Bobby Murkus's nerdy face.

How's that for settling, jerk?

A table lamp was on nearby, casting Drake's face partially in shadow. And Bertie suddenly couldn't breathe. There was so much character in this man. He was so completely compelling.

It was his broad shoulders, the way his hair curled around his baseball cap, the deep brown eyes that had gone hot with arousal. All of it was an intoxicating concoction that melted the last of any resistance she'd had. Even if it was only for tonight, she wanted to be present one hundred percent. She gave a quick thanks to the universe that she'd sobered up.

Because she had to face it: she didn't get opportunities like this every day.

"What did that little twerp mean by 'arrangement'?" Drake's gravelly voice cut through the quiet.

His question only succeeded in driving further home just how unusual this moment was for her. It was all a little humiliating, honestly. She tried to back away, but he reached out and placed his hands on her hips, stopping her. And there was no way she could have walked away from the feel of his hands on her even if she tried.

With her heart beating heavily, she relented. "Bobby thinks we should be 'settle partners.' "

Drake's brow shot up. "What in hell does that mean?" His hands flexed on her hips gently and she had to resist the urge to sigh blissfully at the heat his palms gave off.

It was hard admitting such a thing to anyone, much less the man of her dreams. It was like saying, *I'm a bottom feeder not worthy of your crumbs. So is Bobby. He thinks we deserve each other and wants to get hitched.* Okay, so maybe a little less painful than that, but still.

It sucked.

And it made her wonder what Drake even saw in her.

Talk about a mood killer. "It means he thinks I'm the settling kind and that I should choose him because he's as good as I'm gonna get."

His reaction wasn't what she expected. One of his hands cupped her cheek and he lowered his face down to hers. Until she couldn't look anywhere but at his beautiful brown eyes. "Listen to me. You're smart and insightful and have a wicked sense of humor. He's an ass."

Her breath caught. What was he saying? "How do you know?"

Humor sparked in those mahogany depths. "Because I've been doing some reading."

What was that supposed to mean?

The hand cupping her cheek began to slide slowly down her throat, the heat and hardness of his palm creating an erotic dance of sensations along her skin. "I don't understand," she whispered as her head fell back to give him better access. An ache flared low in her belly and spread down, pooling between her legs.

His mouth replaced his hand, his lips teasing softly. "Neither of us is what we seem, sweet thing."

It was like he was speaking in code. But before she could even try to decrypt it, his mouth was on hers and then she didn't care if he was speaking Martian. All that mattered was the way his lips moved over hers, so sure and coaxing.

Tipping her head all the way back, Bertie gave in to the need and kissed him in return, her lips parting under his. His groan made her bolder and her tongue met his, tangled. He tasted of Cristal and something dark— something intoxicatingly male.

Sinking into the decadence of it, Bertie ran her hands over the dips and planes of his fit body. When her fingers found the hem of his T-shirt, she tugged at it until her hand could slide against his flat, bare abdomen. His quick inhale made her feel sexy and powerful.

It was an incredible feeling, knowing she turned Drake on. And it went straight to her head faster than an entire bottle of Cristal. Oh, how she loved it.

DRAKE FELT THE change in Bertie the moment it happened. She went from shy to sultry in a blink, and it had desire sparking like a wildfire inside him. Her lush little body melted against him, opened, invited him in.

He didn't have to be told twice.

Picking her up like she weighed nothing, he covered

her protest with a hot, searching kiss as he navigated his way down the hall to his bedroom, flicking on a light as he went. Once they were inside he laid her on the moss-green comforter and lowered himself slowly over her. In the semidarkness her eyes shimmered and her full lips looked as juicy as ripe berries.

He had to taste her.

For two years he'd wondered about the woman who'd captivated him with her sharp mind and big heart, and now she was here in the flesh, perfect in every single way even if she didn't think so. It filled him with up with emotions and something a lot like hope. What had he done to deserve this?

Hell if he knew. But he wasn't going to waste this chance to show Bertie how he felt. Lowering his head to her chest, he trailed kisses along the damp collar of her shirt until he came to the valley between her breasts. Stopping there, he inhaled the sweet scent of her skin and Cristal.

It made him so damn hungry. For her.

On a low growl, Drake opened his mouth and trailed his tongue slowly, lightly between her full, gorgeous breasts. When she gasped and arched into his mouth, he slid his tongue between them again, the taste of champagne on her skin driving him crazy with need.

For so long he'd allowed himself to be distracted by superficiality—by women with nothing more to offer than their looks. And in all that time he'd never been as turned on as he was at that moment by one short, brainy brunette. "You taste so good, girl," he whispered against her skin as he licked and kissed the swell of her breasts.

Bertie raised her head, her hands roaming leisurely over his body, and smiled down at him softly. "Really?"

Drake looked up and stilled. He'd never seen anything more beautiful than her at that moment.

Overcome with the emotion, Drake rose up and took her mouth in a passionate, soul-searing kiss. He lost himself in the taste and feel of her, needing to know her every nuance. And it was like coming home.

Breaking the kiss, Bertie pulled back and sucked in air. Then she was yanking his ball cap off and saying in a voice gone throaty with arousal, "You have too many clothes on."

Drake laughed softly and nipped her chin before pulling back to remove his flannel shirt. "Same goes for you. Take it all off."

They took their time removing each other's clothes, touching and caressing as they went. It was like they both wanted to savor the moment, the reality of what was happening. Tracing his fingertips along the dips and curves of her beautiful body, his breathing became ragged with anticipation as she quivered beneath him. She moaned quietly and it made his stomach knot with desire. He sat at the side of the bed and took her in, every breathtaking inch of her. Just as she began to lie back down on the mattress, he grabbed her around the waist and lifted her, settling her on his lap facing him. His cock rubbed intimately against her wet folds and when she shifted, settling more fully, her beautiful pussy brushed the length of him and he dropped his forehead to hers groaning, "God, Bertie."

Then his hands were around her slender waist and he was tonguing her nipple hungrily, murmuring his approval when it grew instantly hard. She moaned and dove her fingers into his hair, holding him to her. Wanting to drive her wild, he covered her nipple with his mouth and sucked, his teeth tugging gently.

Her hands fisted in his hair and she cried out softly, "Drake!"

Completely in the moment, he whispered against her skin, "What is it, love?"

Rocking against him, she found his mouth and kissed him hard. "I need to have you in me."

"Are you sure?" he asked, even though he could feel the evidence of her desire for him against his cock. He just needed to hear her say those words again.

His hand slipped between her legs and when he found her he slid a finger along her lips, loving how wet she was for him. When he found her clit he began rubbing it gently, circling slowly until she bucked against him and demanded, "In me now!"

Needing that too, Drake reached for the nightstand and fumbled for protection. Taking it from him, Bertie put it on quickly and then lowered herself onto him, enveloping him with her moist heat. "Jesus." He gasped.

A thoroughly female smile cupped her lips as she began to move, a slow, steady grind on him that brought him close to the edge so fast he had to hold her still so he could calm down. But she wasn't having any of it. Lost in her own world of sensation, Bertie rode him harder and faster, until he didn't think he could hold out anymore, until he was panting and wrapping his arms around her, her lush warm body his lifeline.

And then she came. On an explosion so forceful it pushed him over the edge and he climaxed so hard it ripped a groan from his chest and he cried out, "Roberta!"

For several long minutes they clung to each other in the semidarkness, their heavy breathing the only sound in the room. And he sat there with his mind reeling over what had just happened. Because never, not once in his thirty-five years, had he ever felt like that with a woman. That close and open, that intimate. Like they were two halves of a whole.

It was beautiful and humbling.

Bertie's head had dropped to his shoulder and Drake brushed a clump of her hair aside so he could kiss her temple. "How you doing there, baby?" he asked quietly against her temple. He could still feel little tremors of aftershock run through her boneless body every so often.

"*So* good," she mumbled lazily against his neck.

That's what he wanted to hear. Affection for her filled him and warmed his chest. Wrapping his arms around her, Drake hugged her and lowered them both gently onto the bed. "You ready for bed, sweetheart?" he asked. Her breathing had started to slow and even out.

Tucking her against him, he pulled a corner of the bedspread over them and whispered, "Good night, Roberta." Then he smiled because he'd just discovered something. Falling asleep with Bertie by his side didn't just feel good.

It felt right.

Chapter Six

BERTIE WOKE THE next morning with panic lodged in her chest. *He knows*, was all she could think. And she couldn't get away from Drake fast enough.

Easing out from under his arm, she untangled herself from the bedsheets and slipped ungracefully from the bed. In the darkness of predawn she fumbled for her clothes, listening for any change in Drake's breathing, for an indication that he was waking. But the man was out cold and snoring softly.

Part of her felt thrilled about that. They'd come together three times during the night, the last time so tender and intimate that she'd actually cried. Drake had taken her places she'd only imagined existed.

It had been the best night of her life.

And now it was all ruined. Because he had figured

out who she really was. It hadn't registered when he'd first said it. Oh no, it had taken until about three in the morning, right after their last steamy encounter. She'd just been dozing off to sleep when she it came to her that he'd called her Roberta. And she'd freaked out then. But the feel of his large body, so warm and solid and naked against her had proven her undoing and she'd fallen into such a sound sleep, she was still a little embarrassed.

But not nearly as embarrassed as she was that Drake had figured her out, which meant he also knew about her secret crush on him. He knew *everything*. By his own admission he read her comic strip. How was she ever supposed to face him now?

Good God, how long had he known? Had it been all along and this was just some kind of joke? Some sort of game?

Did he think it was *funny*, sleeping with the girl who had the pathetically huge crush on him?

Feeling sick to her stomach, Bertie gathered her clothes and silently padded barefoot out of his room. She didn't stop until she was at the front door and had to either get dressed or chance someone seeing her dash across the hall to her apartment naked. Neither option was too appealing. If she took the time to get dressed, then she might make a noise that would wake Drake up. But if she didn't, well, then there was the whole someone-seeing-her-naked-bits thing.

The fear of him waking combined with her current level of mortification had her turning the doorknob without a stitch of clothing on. She was willing to risk it. Until she figured out what to do and how to feel about everything, she needed space. And time to think.

Poking her head into the hall, Bertie looked both ways. Seeing no one, she took a deep breath, held her clothes to her chest, and made a dash for it.

DRAKE HEARD THE door close and opened his eyes, feeling relaxed and well rested. His good feeling disappeared in an instant when he discovered he was in bed alone. What the hell?

Throwing back the covers, he sat up and scrubbed his hands over his face. He knew the sound of his front door shutting. Should he go after Bertie? It stung, knowing she'd left without a word. Last night had been incredible—amazing even. The woman of his dreams had been in his arms, warm and wet with arousal for him. This morning all he got was the sound of the door clicking shut behind her as if she couldn't wait to bail.

Part of him wanted to be really pissed off. Okay, most of him did. But this was Bertie. He knew by her comic strip that she wasn't the love 'em and leave 'em type. She was the love 'em forever kind. So what was her deal?

Drake stretched his arms over his head and yawned loudly. The sound was like a thunder clap in the quiet early morning. Since she wasn't the casual type, maybe she was embarrassed by what had happened. There'd been no courtship, no dating.

Hell, there'd been no wooing at all.

Drake grinned suddenly. That was it! Bertie needed

wooing. She needed him to show her that he was serious about this thing they'd discovered. No way was she just another one of his women, as she'd so delicately put it. She was special, and as he'd discovered last night, full of surprises.

God, he still couldn't believe she was Roberta C. His crush. But as much as he loved the idea of her, the flesh-and-blood woman he'd held in his arms was more complex and way more intriguing. That's who he wanted.

Drake thought about her comic strip.

And suddenly he knew just how to woo her.

BERTIE DARTED ACROSS the hall only to realize she was still locked out. "Son of a bitch!"

Rolling her eyes to the ceiling, Bertie stretched onto her tiptoes and reached above her head with a hand. Feeling along the top of the door frame, she sighed audibly when her fingers encountered a key. It was a spare one to the front door that she'd kept up there for emergencies since the day she'd moved in.

Why in the hell hadn't she remembered it last night?

"Because you're an idiot, Bertie," she grumbled as she quickly unlocked her door and went inside. Relief flooded her at the sight of all her familiar things. It looked right. Normal. Like she hadn't lost her head and slept with her dream man, only to realize after the fact that he'd probably known about her obsession with him all along and was just having fun at her expense. It made sense to her now. The comment he'd made yesterday morning about how he thought Bonnie having the hots for the ballplayer was so damn funny was clearly his giveaway, now that she thought about it. He obviously knew her secret. Good God, maybe he thought she was the ultimate groupie and he was just humoring her!

Because really, why else would Drake have come on to her in the first place? Especially when there were so many other women just waiting for a chance at him.

And why did the thought of him not being serious about her hurt so bad?

Probably because if he wasn't serious about her, then maybe Bobby really was right. Maybe men like Drake saw her for one thing only: amusement.

He'd probably thought it would be a great story to tell his teammates during their next road trip. Yeah, something that would give them all a good laugh. A little tale about the plain Jane who lived across the hall and spent most of her time pining for him through her comic-strip character.

Oh God, what if he thought she'd actually broken into his apartment and sniffed every pair of his underwear, pocketing a few—just because Bonnie had?

Bertie shuffled into the bedroom and flung herself across her bed. *Just kill me now.* Right now, when the humiliation and embarrassment she was feeling slightly edged out her heartache. "Ugh!" She pounded her fists into the mattress. It would be right in line with her life to fall hopelessly in love with a man who saw her only as someone to laugh at.

But then why had he looked at her like the sun rose and set in her eyes?

It just didn't make any sense. The only thing she was sure of was that she never wanted to speak to Drake again. They'd had one good—no, make that *incredible*—night together. And that was great. But now she was going to have to move, because knowing that he knew her whole sordid secret made the idea of running into him on a semi-regular basis absolutely unacceptable.

No way could she live like that.

Pressure built in her chest making it hurt. Grabbing a pillow, Bertie shoved her face into it and screamed. Once. Twice. Three times. When she was done, she raised her head and thumped a fist repeatedly into the center of the pillow. "Why, why, *why*?"

Was it really too much to ask for the universe to just give her someone to love?

Maybe more to the point, for someone to love her?

Deciding she'd wallowed enough, Bertie crawled naked up her bed and dove under the covers. A few days' sleep should help her feel better. If that wasn't enough, she'd try a few more.

Closing her eyes, she tried to sleep, but Drake's scent was all over her. Part of her wanted to inhale so deep that his smell would be permanently imprinted into her memory. The other part wanted to shower in really, really hot water until there was nothing left to remind her of him and their night together.

In the end she compromised. She showered and put

on her favorite flannel pajamas, but she didn't put her shirt from the night before in the laundry pile. Instead, she balled it up and shoved it under her pillow so that only the teeniest bit of his scent was released. *If* she was inclined to smell it—which she wasn't. She was feeling sentimental, that's all.

Whether that was the case or not, Bertie fell asleep with her hand under her pillow, her fingers curled around the soft cotton T-shirt. She woke a few hours later to the sound of someone knocking on her door.

"I know you're in there, Bertie. Open up."

She sat bolt upright. It was Drake. And he didn't sound happy. In fact, he sounded downright surly.

Still feeling fuzzy headed from sleep, she climbed out of bed and padded barefoot to the front door. Stretching up on her tiptoes until she could see through the peep-hole, Bertie felt her heart falter at the sight of him. His hat was back on, his crazy hair curling wildly beneath it. A dark stubble-beard covered his strong jaw and he had on another flannel over his T-shirt—this one a blue plaid.

Drake looked rugged and gorgeous, and he really just needed to go away. She wasn't up for any more humiliation. "Go away, Paulson!"

Through the tiny hole she watched him frown. "Why would I do that?" he asked loudly back, his tone a mixture of frustration and confusion. Did she really have to spell it out for him? What was he doing there anyway?

"If you've come to gloat you've wasted your time."

"What are you talking about?" he practically shouted, his frown turning fierce. "Do you have any idea what it felt like to wake up alone after last night? Why did you bail on me?"

"*Shhh.* Keep it down! You'll wake the neighbors," she chided. Emotions crashed through her, one after the other, and being bossy helped her regain some control.

Drake sighed, long and heartfelt. "What am I supposedly gloating about, Bertie?"

"That you figured me out! That you nailed the comic writer with the big crush on you, you jerk. Whatever. Take your pick!" Even just saying the words stung. It was so embarrassing. How could she for a moment have thought he was serious about her?

"Is that why you disappeared this morning?" He asked through the door. "Because you're embarrassed that I know about your secret crush on me?"

The way he said it made it all sound so juvenile. Couldn't he see it was far more serious than that? Bertie went on the defensive. "How long have you known, huh? How long have you been laughing at me behind my back?" Then a thought occurred to her. "Did you plan this entire thing, starting with Geoff's party?"

Watching him through the peephole gave her a front-row view as his face changed from confused and a little frustrated to full-on angry. It was impressive, the way his eyebrows slashed so low and his eyes went hot. "Do you honestly think that? Really?"

Still feeling emotionally thin and vulnerable, Bertie retorted, "Why shouldn't I? Before yesterday you didn't even know I existed." The truth of that still hurt.

She didn't think his scowl could get any hotter, but

she was wrong. It became downright scorching. "If that's the way you feel then I guess you won't be wanting these." Drake held up a bouquet of pink and red Gerbera daisies for her to see.

Her heart stumbled. But before she could even unlock the door, he'd set them on the floor and strode back into his apartment. The door shut with a sound click.

"Fine." Bertie said. That just proved that he wasn't serious about her, if he was willing to give up so easily.

Trying hard not to feel brokenhearted, she wandered back into the kitchen and started making coffee. But she couldn't resist the lure of the flowers just waiting for her out in the hall. She picked them up gently off the floor and shoved her nose in them, inhaling deeply. Moving back through her apartment, she admired the arrangement and put them in a vase of water on her counter.

Then she turned back to cooking. Once she started puttering around she really got into things. Next thing she knew she was whipping up a batch of waffles and frying bacon.

By the time the coffee had finished, the kitchen was filled with many wonderful aromas and Bertie had successfully distracted herself from herself. Cooking was handy that way.

The last waffle had just come out of the iron when the doorbell rang. Wondering who it could be, and only mostly hoping it was Drake, Bertie wiped her hands on a dish towel and went to answer the door.

It was a singing telegram. For Valentine's Day. Just like the one Bonnie had surprised her ballplayer with.

Bertie waited until the oversized Cupid finished and then promptly shut the door. Only to open it again ten minutes later to a huge box full of chocolates with a picture of her face glued to the box. They were almost exactly like the ones Bonnie had given her secret Valentine.

What on earth was going on?

Three more times over the next few hours the doorbell rang. The first time she opened the door to find a teddy bear wearing an old Rush T-shirt. Instantly her mind flashed to one of her strips when Bonnie had placed a bear wearing one of her shirts in the ballplayer's bed. He'd been having trouble sleeping for days. She'd kept hearing him shuffling around late at night through their shared wall, so she'd snuck in one night and placed it there for him to cuddle with.

Misguided idea and stalker-ish, yes. But Bonnie's heart had been in the right place.

Bertie picked up the bear with the brown curly fur and hugged it to her chest, emotional and confused. She couldn't tell what message Drake was trying to send her. Was he saying he couldn't sleep without her?

On one hand, he could be trying to be cute by sending her the same gift as her alter ego. On the other hand, he could just be rubbing it in and trying to embarrass her.

Though deep down she didn't want to believe that Drake would do such a mean-spirited thing, the doubt was enough to make her stomach hurt. And it didn't get any easier as the day went by and gift after gift kept coming. All of them something out of her comic strip.

The second one was a coffee mug. It was just like the

one Bonnie had given the ballplayer when he'd dropped his cup in the hallway and it had shattered everywhere, little porcelain shards landing on Bonnie's bare feet when she'd been out collecting the paper in the early morning. She'd taken one look at his crestfallen expression and promptly gifted him with her favorite one. In the strip the last frame ended with the huge, masculine player sipping coffee from a dainty mug that was covered in a pink, sparkly unicorn and rainbows. He'd had a big, satisfied smiled on his face.

Was Drake trying to tell her that he was satisfied? Or was this another joke and she was completely missing the punch line?

It gave her a headache trying to figure it out. She'd almost given up when the third gift arrived. It was a pair of jumper cables from the episode when Bonnie had put some on the ballplayer's SUV. She'd placed them on the hood after she'd overheard him telling someone on the phone about how he'd had to catch a cab at two in the morning because his car wouldn't start and he'd lost his cables. She'd been worried sick when she'd heard that he'd been harassed by some thugs while waiting, so much so that buying him new cables was worth her peace of mind.

One of the clamps even had a sticky note attached to it. It read simply:

Understand yet?

She didn't. Not in the least. What was she supposed to understand?

By the time evening rolled around, Bertie had acquired a large pile of gifts and packages. They were all heaped by the front door. She had just sat down to contemplate their meaning for about the thousandth time that day when she heard rustling at the door.

This time the doorbell didn't ring. Instead she watched as something was shoved through her mail slot and landed with a thump on the floor. Curious, Bertie walked over and picked it up.

Shock rooted her to the floor and her mouth dropped open on a "Wha—?"

In her hand was a stack of her comic strips, all cut out and stapled together. Quickly flipping through the clearly worn pages, Bertie saw that nearly all of her comic from the past two years was there. Holes in the upper left-hand corners bore proof that as the stack had grown the pages had been re-stapled many times. The corners were bent and crumpled—some of them even torn.

It had the look of a well-loved book.

Flipping to the last page, Bertie held it with trembling fingers as all the possible meanings and ramifications of this handmade comic book sprang to her mind. Thought after thought spun through her head, but only one of them stuck: Drake had collected her work.

And he had started long ago.

Tears sprang to her eyes and her heart started hammering. Why had Drake kept all of her comics?

"I know you, Bertie Cogswell." His voice came from right on the other side of the door. He must have been standing there the whole time. "I may not have met you face-to-face until yesterday, but I've known you for years. That booklet I made of your comics goes with me pretty much everywhere. I read it on planes, in hotels, and even when I'm home and just want a pick-me-up."

Her voice cracked with emotion when she replied, "What are you saying?"

Cradling the comics to her chest, Bertie looked through the peephole again. And there he was, standing in the middle of the hallway, looking as casual as could be while he said, "I'm saying that I fell for you a long time ago, little mouse. Long before we ever met in person."

Tears stung her eyes and her heart swelled with emotion. There were things she had to ask him, things she needed to be sure about. Fumbling with the locks, Bertie swung the door open and demanded, "Even though I look like this?" She gestured to her gray-and-pink polka-dotted pajama pants and up at her hair. Was he sure about this? She still wore Scrunchies, for crissake.

Drake just raised a brow and replied, "I look like this." The man was unconventionally sexy.

"It's not the same."

He took a step toward her. "Is so, Bertie. Look, I like you for *who* you are. For all your wit and insecurities and your big loving heart. I couldn't help falling for that. It's all right there." He nodded at the stapled comics. "*You're* right there."

She could see the truth of what he was saying. Her heart and soul were poured into her work. Every hope, fear and dream. Drake saw that. More than that, he understood that.

And he wanted her for it.

It was a Valentine's Day miracle.

Suddenly elated and overflowing with affection for her big, burly ballplayer, Bertie launched herself at him knowing full well he'd catch her. And he did. "I really like you, Drake Paulson."

Strong arms pulled her in tight. "I really like you too, Roberta C." He kissed her sweetly and then grinned like the devil. "Or should I call you the Ambush Predator?"

Laughing, she slapped him playfully on the shoulder. "So it's like that, is it?"

He nodded and scooped her up in his arms. "Yeah, it's like that. But don't worry, baby. You caught me."

Epilogue

DRAKE HEARD THE thump at the door and quietly climbed out of bed. Bertie was sacked out next to him and he didn't want to wake her, but he'd been waiting all week to find out how the ballplayer would react to Bonnie's Valentine's gifts, so he made his way through the early-morning dark to grab the paper that'd just arrived. Hopefully the guy had finally wised up and seen the truth. Bonnie was a keeper.

Closing the door behind him, Drake quickly flipped to the comic section. When his eyes landed on her strip, pride for Bertie swelled inside him and his lips curved in a smile. It simply amazed him that she came up with this stuff. She was one incredible woman.

But then he read the comic and his smile turned into a frown of irritation. "Damn it, Bertie!" He called out as he scowled down at the picture of the ballplayer meanly dumping his beloved Bonnie's chocolates in the garbage. "You got it all wrong!"

Drake heaved a great sigh as he headed back to the bedroom. Looked like it was up to him to make her see things his way. A slow smile spread over his face as he crawled back into bed and pulled her in close.

He could do that. Yeah, he could do that real good.

If you enjoyed Drake and Bertie's
story, see where it all began
for the ballplayers of Jennifer Seasons's sexy
Diamonds and Dugouts series!

STEALING HOME

PLAYING THE FIELD

THROWING HEAT

Available now from Avon Impulse

JENNIFER SEASONS is a Colorado transplant. She lives with her husband and four children along the Front Range, where she enjoys breathtaking views of the mighty Rocky Mountains every day. A dog and two cats keep them company. When she's not writing, she loves spending time with her family outdoors, exploring her beautiful adopted home state.

Visit www.AuthorTracker.com for exclusive information on your favorite HarperCollins authors.

Give in to your impulses . . .
Read on for a sneak peek at four brand-new
e-book original tales of romance
from Avon Books.
Available now wherever e-books are sold.

THE LAST WICKED SCOUNDREL
A SCOUNDRELS OF ST. JAMES NOVELLA
By Lorraine Heath

BLITZING EMILY
A LOVE AND FOOTBALL NOVEL
By Julie Brannagh

SAVOR
A BILLIONAIRE BACHELORS CLUB NOVEL
By Monica Murphy

IF YOU ONLY KNEW
A TRUST NO ONE NOVEL
By Dixie Lee Brown

An Excerpt from

THE LAST WICKED SCOUNDREL
A Scoundrels of St. James Novella
by Lorraine Heath

New York Times and *USA Today* bestselling author
Lorraine Heath brings us the eagerly awaited
final story in the Scoundrels of St. James series.

Winnie, the Duchess of Avendale, never knew
peace until her brutal husband died. With
William Graves, a royal physician, she's discovered
burning desire—and the healing power of love.
But now, confronted by the past she thought she'd
left behind, Winnie must face her fears . . . or risk
losing the one man who can fulfill all her dreams.

After last night, she'd dared to hope that she meant something special to him, but they were so very different in rank and purpose. She considered suggesting that they go for a walk now, but she didn't want to move away from where she was. So near to him. He smelled of sandalwood. His jaw and cheeks were smooth. He'd shaved before he came to see her. His hair curled wildly about his head, and she wondered if he ever tried to tame it, then decided he wouldn't look like himself without the wildness.

With his thumb, he stroked her lower lip. His blue eyes darkened. She watched the muscles of his throat work as he swallowed. Leaning in, he lowered his mouth to hers. She rose up on her toes to meet him, inviting him to possess, plunder, have his way. She became lost in the sensations of his mouth playing over hers, vaguely aware of his twisting her around so they were facing each other. As she skimmed her hands up over his shoulders, his arms came around her, drawing her nearer. He was a man of nimble fingers, skilled hands that eased hurts and injuries and warded off death. He had mended her with those hands, and now with his lips he was mending her further.

Suddenly changing the angle of his mouth, he deepened

the kiss, his tongue hungrily exploring, enticing her to take her own journey of discovery. He tasted of peppermint. She could well imagine him keeping the hard candies in his pocket to hand to children in order to ease their fears. Snitching one for himself every now and then.

He folded his hands around the sides of her waist and, without breaking his mouth from hers, lifted her onto the desk. Parchment crackled beneath her. She knew she should be worried that they were ruining the plans for the hospital, but she seemed unable to care about anything beyond the wondrous sensations that he was bringing to life.

Avendale had never kissed her with such enthusiasm, such resolve. She felt as though William were determined to devour her, and that it would be one of the most wondrous experiences of her life.

Hiking her skirts up over her knees, he wedged himself between her thighs. Very slowly, he lowered her back to the desk until she was sprawled over it like some wanton. On the desk! She had never known this sort of activity could occur anywhere other than the bed. It was wicked, exciting, intriguing. Surely he didn't mean to do more than kiss her, not that she was opposed to him going further.

She'd gone so long without a caress, without being desired, without having passions stirred. She felt at once terrified and joyful while pleasure curled through her.

As he dragged his mouth along her throat, he began undoing buttons, giving himself access to more skin. He nipped at her collarbone, circled his tongue in the hollow at her throat. She plowed her fingers through his golden locks, relishing the soft curls as they wound around her fingers.

More buttons were unfastened. She sighed as he trailed his mouth and tongue along the upper swells of her breasts. Heat pooled deep within her. She wrapped her legs around his hips, taking surcease from the pressure of him against her. He moaned low, more a growl than anything as he pressed a kiss in the dip between her breasts.

God help her, but she wanted to feel his touch over all of her.

Peeling back her bodice, he began loosening the ribbons on her chemise. In the distance, someplace far far away, she thought she heard a door open.

"The count—" Her butler began and stopped.

"Winnie?" Catherine's voice brought her crashing back to reality.

An Excerpt from

BLITZING EMILY
A Love and Football Novel
by Julie Brannagh

All's fair in Love and Football . . .

Emily Hamilton doesn't trust men. She's much
more comfortable playing the romantic lead
in front of a packed house onstage than in her
own life. So when NFL star and alluring ladies'
man Brandon McKenna acts as her personal
white knight, she has no illusions that he'll
stick around. However, a misunderstanding
with the press throws them together in a
fake engagement that yields unexpected (and
breathtaking) benefits in the first installment
of Julie Brannagh's irresistible new series.

Emily had barely enough time to hang up the cordless and flip on the TV before Brandon wandered down the stairs.

"Hey," he said, and he threw himself down on the couch next to her.

His blond curls were tangled, his eyes sleepy, and she saw a pillowcase crease on his cheek. He looked completely innocent, until she saw the wicked twinkle in his eyes. Even in dirty workout clothes, he was breathtaking. She wondered if it was possible to ovulate on demand.

"I'm guessing you took a nap," she said.

"I was supposed to be watching you." He tried to look penitent. It wasn't working.

"Glad to know you're making yourself comfortable," she teased.

He stretched his arm around the back of the couch.

"Everything in your room smells like flowers, and your bed's great." He pulled up the edge of his t-shirt and sniffed it. Emily almost drooled at a glimpse of his rock-hard abdomen. Evidently, it was possible to have more than a six pack. "The guys will love my new perfume. Maybe they'll want some makeup tips," he muttered, and grabbed for the remote Emily left on the coffee table.

He clicked through the channels at a rapid pace.

"Excuse me. I had that." She lunged for it. No such luck. Emily ended up sprawled across his lap.

"The operative word here, sugar, is 'had.'" He held it up in the air out of her reach while he continued to click. He'd wear a hole in his thumb if he kept this up. "No NFL Network." She tried to sit up again, which wasn't working well. Of course, he was chuckling at her struggles. "Oh, I get it. You're heading for second base."

"Hardly." Emily reached over and tried to push off on the other arm of the couch. One beefy arm wrapped around her. "I'm not trying to do anything. Oh, whatever."

"You know, if you want a kiss, all you have to do is ask."

She couldn't imagine how he managed to look so innocent while smirking.

"I haven't had a woman throw herself in my lap for a while now. This could be interesting," he said.

Emily's eyebrows shot to her hairline. "I did not throw myself in your lap."

"Could've fooled me. Which one of us is—"

"Let go of me." She was still trying to grab the remote, without success.

"You'll fall," he warned.

"What's your point?"

"Here." He stuck the remote down the side of the couch cushion so Emily couldn't grab it. He grasped her upper arms, righted her with no effort at all, and looked into her eyes. "All better. Shouldn't you be resting, anyway?"

Emily tried to take a breath. Their bodies were frozen. He held her, and she gazed into his face. His dimple appeared, vanished, appeared again. She licked her lips with the microscopic amount of moisture left in her mouth. He was fighting a smile, but even more, he dipped his head toward her. He was going to kiss her.

"Yes," she said.

Her voice sounded weak, but it was all she could do to push it out of lungs that had no air at all. He continued to watch her, and he gradually moved closer. Their mouths were inches apart. Emily couldn't stop looking at his lips. After a few moments that seemed like an eternity, he released her and dug the remote from the couch cushion. She felt a stab of disappointment. He had changed his mind.

"Turns out you have the NFL Network, so I think I can handle another twenty-four hours here," he announced as he stopped on a channel she'd never seen before.

"You might not be here another twenty-four minutes. Don't you have a TV at home?" She wrapped her arms around her midsection. She wished she could come up with something more witty and cutting to say. She was so sure he would kiss her, and then he hadn't.

An Excerpt from

SAVOR
A Billionaire Bachelors Club Novel
by Monica Murphy

New York Times bestselling author
Monica Murphy concludes her sexy
Billionaire Bachelors Club series with a fiery
romance that refuses to be left at the office.

Bryn James can't take much more of being invisible
to her smart, sexy boss, Matthew DeLuca.
Matt's never been immune to his gorgeous
assistant's charms, and though he's tried to
stay professional, Bryn—with a jaw-dropping
new look—is suddenly making it very difficult.
And when the lines between business and
pleasure become blurred, he'll be faced with
the biggest risk of his career—and his heart.

Bryn

"I shouldn't do this." He's coming right at me, one determined step after another, and I slowly start to back up, fear and excitement bubbling up inside me, making it hard to think clearly.

"Shouldn't do what?"

I lift my chin, my gaze meeting his, and I see all the turbulent, confusing emotions in his eyes, the grim set of his jaw and usually lush mouth. The man means business—what sort of business I'm not exactly sure, but I can take a guess. Increasing my pace, I take hurried backward steps to get away from all that handsome intensity coming at me until my butt meets the wall.

I'm trapped. And in the best possible place too.

"You've been driving me fucking crazy all night," he practically growls, stopping just in front of me.

I have? I want to ask, but I keep my lips clamped tight. He never seems to notice me, not that I ever really want him to. Or at least, that's what I tell myself. That sort of thing usually brings too much unwanted attention. I've dealt with that sort of trouble before, and it nearly destroyed me.

The more time I spend with my boss though, the more I want him to see me. Really see me as a woman. Not the dependable, efficiently organized Miss James who makes his life so much easier.

I want Matt to see me as a woman. A woman he wants.

Playing with fire. . .

The thought floating through my brain is apt, considering the potent heat in Matt's gaze.

"I don't understand how I could be, considering I've done nothing but work my tail off the entire evening," I retort, wincing the moment the words leave me. I blame my mounting frustration over our situation. I'm tired, I've done nothing but live and breathe this winery opening for the last few weeks, and I'm ready to go home and crawl into bed. Pull the covers over my head and sleep for a month.

But if a certain someone wanted to join me in my bed, there wouldn't be any sleeping involved. Just plenty of nakedness and kissing and hot, delicious sex . . .

My entire body flushes at the thought.

"And I appreciate you working that pretty tail of yours off for me. Though I'd hate to see it go," he drawls, his gaze dropping low. Like he's actually trying to check out my backside. His flirtatious tone shocks me, rendering me still.

Our relationship isn't like this. Strictly professional is how Matt and I keep it between us. But that last remark was most definitely what I would consider flirting. And the way he's looking at me . . .

Oh. My.

My cheeks warm when he stops directly in front of me. I

can feel his body heat, smell his intoxicating scent, and I press my lips together to keep from saying something really stupid.

God, I want you. So bad my entire body aches for your touch.

Yeah. I sound like those romance novels I used to devour when I had more time to freaking read. I always thought those emotions were so exaggerated. No way could what happens in a romance novel actually occur in real life.

But I'm feeling it. Right now. With Matthew DeLuca. And the way he's looking at me almost makes me think he might be feeling it too.

"So um, h-how have I been driving you crazy?" I swallow hard. I sound like a stuttering idiot, and I'm trying to calm my racing heart but it's no use. We're staring at each other in silence, the only sound our accelerated breathing, and then he reaches out. Rests his fingers against my cheek. Lets them drift along my face.

Slowly I close my eyes and part my lips, sharp pleasure piercing through me at his intimate touch. I curl my fingers against the wall as if I can grab onto it, afraid I might slide to the ground if I don't get a grip and soon. I can smell him. Feel him. We've been close to each other before, but not like this. Never like this.

An Excerpt from

IF YOU ONLY KNEW
A Trust No One Novel
by Dixie Lee Brown

Beautiful and deadly, Rayna Dugan is a force to
be reckoned with. But when she must suddenly
defend her life against a criminal empire, Rayna
knows she needs backup. Ex-cop Ty Whitlock
never meant for his former flame to get mixed
up in this mess—a mess he feels responsible for.
Now he's got only one choice: find Rayna and
keep her safe. But that's the easy part. Once
he finds her, can he convince her to stay?

He leaned close. "Goddammit, Rayna. You could have been killed." He breathed the words, and the anger in his expression morphed into fear as he grabbed her forearms and gave her a shake.

The deep emotion playing across his face tugged at her heart. His tortured gaze held her transfixed. She searched for the words to fix everything, starting with the way she'd botched their relationship, but some things couldn't be fixed.

She hooked her fingers through his belt loops and drew semicircles on his firmly toned abdomen with her thumbs until she found her voice again. "But I wasn't . . . thanks to you and Ribs."

Ty straightened and glanced upward, away from her face. "I thought I was going to lose you. I *won't* lose you, Rayna." His piercing gaze fastened on her again, and he raised one hand to caress her cheek. "Don't you get it? We're a team. I *need* you, and whether you'll admit it or not, you need me too."

Hope flared within her at his words, followed almost immediately by a spark of anger. "If you truly believed that, you wouldn't be trying to keep me out of the hunt for Andre. If we're such a good team, why not act like one?"

Ty swept a hand across the back of his neck. "I'm not

trying to keep you . . ." He stopped and looked away from her. "Shit. You're right. I wanted you out of it so you'd be safe, and so I could do my job without worrying about you. I still want you to be safe . . . but I'm fairly certain Joe was going to side with you anyway." He swung his gaze back to her, and amusement quirked his lips. "Besides, if he takes you home, you'll just spend all your time worrying about me."

"Oh, you think so?" Rayna raised a quizzical eyebrow. Did he mean it this time? Would he let her help take Andre down, or was he simply putting her off again?

Ty grew serious. "Stay with me, Rayna, and we'll get this guy. He won't know what hit him."

His soft words and the sincerity in his eyes melted her heart and filled her with sadness at the same time. It sounded like he was asking her to stay with him forever, but he'd already made it clear that he wasn't returning to Montana. So where did that leave them? The smart thing to do would be to ask, but her courage failed in the face of what his answer could be. For right now, she wanted to believe he meant forever, but the truth was she wanted him for however long he would have her, and she'd convince him later that he couldn't live without her. Did that make her desperate? So what if it did? She grabbed a fistful of his shirt and pulled him closer as she shook her head slowly. "Try getting rid of me."

A genuine smile lit his eyes, and his head lowered slowly. His lips touched hers in a lingering kiss, warm and promising more. His arms slid around her waist, pulled her in tightly, and he rested his chin on top of her head. She inhaled a deep breath, and her wild heartbeat began to slow. The safety and comfort of his embrace was exactly what she needed, and it was surprisingly easy to surrender herself to his care. Of course, there were still things to do. They had to get Ribs back and his wounds treated, but for now—for just a moment . . .

A shrill siren screeched in the distance, disturbing the peace of Nate's uncle's property. Ty tensed and raised his head, listening, then pulled his gun from its shoulder holster.